CW00551299

Also By Onia Fox:

Covid Blues And Twos (Jessica Taylor) – Lockdown Erotica

Alexa – humorous, coming of age, short story

Listless In Turkey

By

Onia Fox

Jessica has a few balls to juggle, both at home and at work, as her personal life unravels in the spring of 2016. To put some order to the chaos, and with the help of her best friend, a bowl of noodles and a second bottle of Pinot, Jessica writes another list – a plan for her future.

The list becomes a self-fulfilling prophecy, safely folded into her journal as she romps across Europe before stumbling into the unfolding Turkish Military Coup.

Be careful for what you wish

Contents

CHAPTER 1 – NEW LIFE

Jessica felt quite pleased with herself, managing to force open one eye. This was not going to be a day of high achieving. Rather than push her luck by trying to open the second eye, she decided to hedge-her-bets – by closing her first eye again. In self-imposed darkness and solitude, Jessica attempted to drift back to sleep to the rhythmic throbbing of her hangover.

Not on a school day

She eventually rolled on to her back, letting an arm flop across the bed. Not looking for conversation and certainly nothing more intimate – nothing that involved any motion – she just wanted to feel Chris's skin. There was no Chris.

Sitting slowly and hanging her head down onto her chest, Jessica began reconstructing her life in her mind. She had started drinking late afternoon from work, outside the bar opposite her flat with a friend from the office. A birthday-eve drink. During the period after Stacy left and before Chris arrived, she consumed another three drinks bought for her by three American marines, sat at the neighbouring table. The four moved inside the bar, just as the May sun dipped. Jessica had an eye for a dashing uniform, especially when filled with muscle and good looks.

Jessica groaned aloud in discomfort, the noise making her start.

Chris arrived around eight and she barely looked at him, continuing to chat with her new friends. They were all so young, handsome, and polite. One was black, one was white and one was mixed-heritage. It felt she was flirting in a Benetton advert.

The marines made perfect gentlemen, standing to leave at around nine-thirty; they were due to sail on the morning high-tide. They shook hands with Jessica and Chris. The white guy even saluted Chris and the mixed-heritage marine bent to kiss Jessica on both cheeks.

So pretty

And then things deteriorated. Chris wanted to go home to Jessica's flat. Jessica wanted to go clubbing at nine-thirty on a Tuesday evening. She tried to make a case but her words were less than coherent. She called Chris boring; he called her flighty, *who says flighty nowadays?* She eventually followed him across the road to her flat, shouting obscenities. Other than that, it had been a nice evening. That was all she could remember – next she was trying to wake up, sit up, open her eyes, and not vomit; she could multi-task as well as the next girl.

Jessica managed to shower, open her secure work laptop, and fire off the three non time-critical emails stored in her outbox for just such an emergency. The team would assume she was working from home. She planned to head to the office, just as soon as she stopped reeking of brandy.

Climbing onto her balcony – or the flat roof of the kitchen below as it was - Jessica walked to the edge and watched her neighbour and friend, nursing and singing to her newborn. She sat in the morning sun with the baby swaddled against the cool air – just a blanket with a pair of sucking lips.

'Hey! How's my beautiful goddaughter and her gorgeous mum?'

'Morning Jess, no work? And why is your chest bright red and your face kind of... puce green? I should take a step back from the edge if I was you.'

'Oh don't Cath. I had a couple last night, I am not feeling brilliant.'

'Chris with you?'

10

'No, he sort of, didn't stay last night. Had to get back.' Cath held her friend's gaze. 'Shit Cath, were we arguing?'

Cathy swapped sides with the baby. 'Well, let's just say baby learned a few new words last night, through the ceiling.'

'Cath, I am really sorry. It won't happen again, promise.'

Peter came out of the kitchen with a mug of tea for his wife and looked up at Jessica; she pulled down her T-shirt to cover herself.

With a grin, Peter offered 'Good morning neighbour, and here's winking straight back at you!'

Cathy slapped her husband's arm and told him to leave Jessica alone. Jessica took the opportunity to shake her head and walk back to the window, shaking her bottom playfully at her friends as she climbed back into her flat. She wished she had not shaken her head, or wiggled her hips, or had brandy in her Prosecco last night.

Taking her second coffee of the morning into the tiny living area, Jessica eased herself on to the small sofa and swiped open the work iPhone. Her friend, also unofficial mentor and senior colleague, had left several texts for her. One was a happy birthday message – the rest were work-related. Amara and Jessica had been lovers briefly, and although they were still extremely close, Jessica was very much aware and respectful of Amara's seniority at work. Amara answered on the second ring.

'Mrs Pebbles! How are you this morning?'

'Don't *Mrs Pebbles* me, Jessica. Where are you?'

'I've just finished some reading for one of my projects. I will be in soon, what's the problem?'

'Stacy said you have missed your team meeting. What the fuck, Jess? I've covered for you, again, but I want you in, now.'

'I can't Am, sorry. I've got a bit of a tummy ache and I've had a brandy to settle it. I'll be in after lunch promise. Look, I'm really sorry…' the line died.

Jessica looked around her tiny flat. She loved her flat, loved her neighbours, and loved this part of Southsea – one road back from the beach and just short of Student-Town-Proper. But it was tiny. She was on good money now - perhaps it was time to move, perhaps even buy. She had been

12

seeing Chris for exactly one year; perhaps they should talk about living together. After last night, perhaps they should just concentrate on talking – period.

Chris had been so good for Jessica following her breakup with Richard, but recently she found him overbearing. *From the fire into the frying pan.* And she found him boring. And he thought her "flighty" – Jessica snorted a laugh to herself.

She also loved her work but was less motivated recently. She had taken her foot off the gas but was still respected and liked in the office, and with Amara watching her back, pretty much invincible.

The previous weekend Jessica watched Mama Mia and Shirley Valentine back-to-back in bed – an early birthday present from her nieces. Perhaps it was time to step off the treadmill and live a little. Maybe travel. Maybe find new love, or at least plenty of lust.

So many perhaps and maybes. She wondered if she could even have a mid-life crisis at 31 years old.

In her tiny bedroom, Jessica found her notebook in the tiny cupboard, above her tiny wardrobe, and took it back to her tiny sofa.

She had rescued the book from her father's most recent garage clearance, just before he threw it onto the bonfire. It was an unused Watch Log from his early army career. The cover was thick waxed paper; the pages heavy and perforated at the wide margin and faintly lined. Foolscap, not A4. Jessica opened the blank pages towards the middle of the book and brought it to her nose, inhaling deeply. The smell took her immediately to her childhood – all musk and uniform. The smell of her father's hugs, when he returned from deployment.

The notebook would be her next journal, but she now deployed it early for a good cause. Jessica turned to the inside back page and smoothed it open. Leaving the top line for a title, she wrote sub-headings in a column on the left side, leaving a line space. This would be a *Jessica list – for my new life.*

The pen shook in her hand for a moment. Once she had written in the notebook, it would no longer be the blank canvas.

She wrote four sub-headings to flesh-out later:

Work

Chris

Flat

Travel Europe

CHAPTER 2 - WORK

Jessica answered the door, signing for the letter and placing it on her in-tray (the top of the breadbin) to read later. She needed to find a couple of hours over the weekend to sort outstanding correspondence, renew her overdue rental agreement, restart some bank standing orders, and look at swapping utility providers. Her grumpy landlord had left voice messages and pushed a note through her letterbox concerning an overdue payment – she would transfer the arrears and pay a month in advance, giving her some breathing space to organise bank payments for another year.

She lay on the sofa with her legs dangling over the arm and slept for another thirty minutes. She bathed, brushed her teeth, vomited, brushed her teeth again, felt much better and dressed for work; she would only need to be in the office for a couple of hours before being able to slope-off home. It was a sunny afternoon and her birthday – she might treat herself to a glass of pinot on the way home, to prepare for a chat with Chris. He was, she realised, more patient with her than she was with him.

About to leave the flat, Jessica answered her iPhone.

'Hey, Stace! I've been busy busy today, Mrs Pebbles asked me to look at some stuff. Anyway, I am on my way in.'

'Hello, Jessica. I'm up with HR. Can you pop over before going to the office? Bring your laptop.'

Jessica thought her work friend's voice unusually flat. They had both enjoyed a couple of large glasses of wine after work yesterday; perhaps she was also a little jaded.

'Sure, do I need to prepare anything?'

'Just bring your laptop.'

'Yeah – you said.' Stacy rang off.

Jessica took a Manila folder of cooking recipes from the kitchen shelf and emptied the contents onto the counter. Looking around for a moment, she collected the Watch Log journal and slipped it inside the folder for padding.

Human Resource was located in the adjoining block to her own office. Her security pass permitted access to the main door and reception. From there a security guard walked Jessica to a small waiting room adjoining a large meeting room.

She heard voices from the meeting room, an unseen door open and close, silence, more voices. Then the meeting room door opened and Stacy beckoned Jessica, gesturing to a chair. Two security guards sat by the second door, and two suits sat opposite Jessica. The female suit spoke.

'Thank you for coming in at such short notice Mrs Khan, especially as you are working... offsite... today.'

Jessica placed her laptop and the manila folder onto the desk and held her pen ready, in case she needed to make notes.

'No problem. Always happy to pop into HR, to receive my bonus.' Jessica grinned at her own joke, Stacy looked down at her lap, and the two suits did not react.

'Mrs Khan, bear with me while I explain something to you. Then I will take your questions.' The female placed a large white envelope onto the desk.

'Mrs Khan...'

'Jess, Jessica, Ms, or Miss Not Missus.'

Both suits turned several pages of documents, correcting entries.

'Sorry, Ms Khan. The Company has undergone a small restructure, following the loss of a contract and with some other contracts approaching conclusion, including one of your projects. I regret to inform you, Jessica, that your position has been made redundant.'

Jessica made to speak, but the female continued. 'You do, of course, have statutory rights and protection under employment law. In this envelope is our offer in way of a thank you and in settlement of your employment contract entitlement. It far exceeds the minimum values guaranteed under law. We have arranged for your union representatives to review our offer with you; they are waiting in the next room. In our experience, you will probably be advised to accept our offer. You have 24 hours to agree or reject the offer, after that it will be withdrawn. Any questions?'

'How much notice, when do I go?'

The male leaned forward and spoke softly.

'You are gone, Ms Khan. Stacy has kindly cleared your desk and has your personal belongings here. You will not be going back into your old office, whether or not you accept the offer. You will of course be paid your salary in lieu of notice.'

Jessica was aware of this security procedure and knew not to take it personally. One benefit of working for an international arms manufacturer.

Jessica opened her notebook, located the only page with writing on it and pretended to scan through the entries, buying herself time to consider her options – she had no options. There were only four words on the page; the only four words in the entire book. The top word in the column read "work". She studied it for a moment before carefully adding an adjacent tick. Closing the book, she had decided.

'I have no further questions, thank you.'

Jessica reached for the envelope, ripping it open.

'Ms Khan, please take a moment, talk to your union and read our offer, carefully.'

Jessica quickly scanned the document, looking for where to sign. She did not look at the detail, nor the sums of money and compensation offered. She signed and dated the acceptance and pushed the pack back across the desk, without taking her copy. Picking up the iPhone to text Amara, she realised it was already deactivated. Jessica tossed the iPhone on top of the laptop with her security identification card, probably also deactivated, collected her notebook and smiled at the two suits.

'Ok. Thank you for your time.'

As she walked towards the exit, one of the security guards joined her to escort her from the building.

CHAPTER 3 – CHRIS

Jessica walked back to her flat alone, the sun shining and the sea-air fresh with salt and ozone. She would tidy and clean the flat, her second favourite form of stress therapy, have a look at continuing the list she had started earlier, see if Cathy needed any company or a hand with baby, have a chat with Amara, cook something nice for Chris, and relax. And she really must look at her correspondence and finances – especially now.

Jessica's primary form of stress relief was exercise. She made full use of her discounted gym membership at the University, including the kickboxing class. She received her membership at a most reasonable rate because she shared her postcode with campus, which was a self-proclaimed "good neighbour". However, if her head said no to exercise today, then her stomach screamed it.

Another of her life-coping mechanisms is to compartmentalise her thoughts. Write a list or an entry into her journal and then just *move-on*. By signing the redundancy offer, she had started that process for today's challenge. Tomorrow, she would complete the next item on her most recent list with not so much as a glance back at today's... disappointment.

Within two hours the flat was spotless, everything back in its place and the three rooms smelled like the spring day it was; she even scraped the congealed pieces of carrot from the toilet bowl. She might cook a spicy stir-fry for Chris – she would throw wet vegetables into a hot wok with a splash of wine, flaming and spitting, to impress her lover. Or she might invite him to cook at hers; he loved cooking for Jessica.

The door intercom buzzed, followed immediately by Amara's voice.

'Hey Vanilla! Come give me a hand, I have chocolate.'

Jessica's heart missed a beat; she loved her friend's pet name for her. Amara had called Jessica Vanilla Essence when they both admitted that Jessica was straight and that their brief fling together was just that, brief.

Jessica met Amara halfway up the stairs. The outside door was only closed at nighttime. Amara carried flowers and a cardboard box; Jessica saw chocolates and Prosecco inside the box. She kissed Amara and took the flowers.

'For me?'

'All but one, my love.'

Inside the flat, Amara took the Prosecco and chocolates from the box. Jess took out her copy of the redundancy offer and added it to the top of the breadbin, carrying the remaining few office possessions, in the box, to her bedroom. Back in the kitchen, Amara took one yellow rose from the bunch, wetted kitchen towel and wrapped tinfoil around the stem. She arranged the remaining roses in a glass water jug that she found on the shelf.

'Wow, Amara! You look fabulous. You didn't wear that to work!'

Amara was a few years older than Jessica, tall, curvy and extremely attractive. Her parents were both Nigerian but Jessica had fantasised Amara had the tall, elegant, classical beauty of an Ethiopian Princess. Her eyes sparkled clear against her black skin.

'Why thank you Ms K.' Amara completed a slow turn to show Jessica her short, perfectly fitting, white dress with a blue and green design stitched through the fabric. Jessica noticed the single rose stem.

'Amara, you are going on a date!'

Amara's eyes twinkled brightly, and she broke into a grin. Jessica felt pleased for her friend, but could not help feeling a faint pang of jealousy. She was determined not to show it.

'Well, spill the beans.'

'Ah, you know Jess. Just some kid, only a date.'

Jessica looked at Amara with a sideways slant of her head.

'Ok ok. Look Jess, it is still early days, but I really do like her. I think, you know. I don't know. You know. Maybe a keeper.' The friends hugged for a long moment. Both aware that Amara was taking a step up life's ladder as Jessica seemed to be slipping down a snake.

'Jess, I did not know about today. I couldn't have done much probably, but I would have tried. And I'm not even available to celebrate your birthday, sorry.'

'Hey don't be silly Am. Let's be honest here, maybe I should have been just a little more focused recently. And if I can get hold of Chris, I will have a passionate night in and not have to set the alarm clock for tomorrow.'

'*If* you *can get hold of Chris*? Have you been arguing again? Have you been messing him around again, Jessica?'

'Damn Amara! They used to burn women like you. How do you do that shit?'

'I can read you like a book. Now listen to me here and don't roll your eyes. If you love him, then start showing it. And if you don't, then let him down gently, poor lamb. He's a good guy and he loves you to bits.'

Before Jessica could respond, the doorbell sounded again. Amara grabbed her bag and the single rose.

'Look Vanilla, this is an early supper and I kind of don't want to get lucky tonight. You know, gently gently. If you are around after my date, I'll pop back to see you. I'm staying in a local hotel, anyway.'

Amara lived in Guildford, worked in Portsmouth, and often stayed over – normally on expenses.

The two friends walked downstairs together and met Chris, standing by the open outside door. Jessica and Amara hugged again, and Chris kissed Amara on the cheek before following Jessica back to her flat.

'Chris, lost your key? What's up?'

'I thought you had someone here.'

Jessica held her lover's face with one hand and stared into his eyes. He gulped and looked down.

'Chris?'

'Jess, I really think the world of you and I have so enjoyed our year together.'

'Chris, stop this.'

'I will always be here for you, always. You must believe that. You have been so brave this past year.'

'Chris, wait a minute. I have something I need to tell you.'

'Jess, I am sorry. We are over. Sorry.'

'No Chris, you don't understand, I don't think you mean this. Look, let me say something.'

Chris placed a key on the kitchen counter and turned to go.

'Chris, wait. For one minute. Let me speak.'

The door closed softly behind him.

Jessica took her coffee down to the backyard she shared with neighbours. The yard had been a dump of the landlord's rubbish when she first moved in, including old commercial kitchen equipment - a huge gas cooker and a massive electric bain-marie, covered with a tarpaulin. Jessica often had her sleep disturbed by sailors and local girls hooking up in the yard and on one occasion, she was stopped going down the alley to the front door by a dealer until his customer had finished shooting-up.

Peter and Cathy moved into their flat on a Friday. On the following Saturday morning, a flatbed van pulled onto the double yellow lines and two council workers, from the Portsmouth City Council Yard that Peter managed, loaded the kitchen equipment onto the van and took it away. Two hours later, they returned with a five-gallon drum of paint, a pressure washer, an old rusty gate and hand tools. They proceeded to scrape and clear away the remaining muck, dead rats, syringes, condoms and rubbish from the yard. By Saturday evening, the yard was spotless and the rusty gate fitted to the alleyway. On Sunday morning Jessica joined her new neighbours in the yard to help Cathy paint the brick walls Transport

Yellow whilst Peter repaired patches of concrete, areas of original Victorian tiles, and painted the gate. On the following weekend, the three drove to Homebase to choose and buy garden furniture together. Jessica's home life transformed.

On that Sunday afternoon, Landlord appeared with a *heavy* shouting about his missing property. Peter calmly explained that he could collect it from the council yard within four weeks, or it would be disposed of, the scene less than friendly. Peter opened the gate and the two men started to push in as Peter slammed it shut on the heavy, trapping Landlord. Peter kept his hands by his sides but pushed his face into Landlord's, his chin jutting into Landlord's cheek and his head clattering against the other's eye. Spitting out the words, Peter growled at Landlord, sending phlegm and spittle over his face.

'You ever come round to my home again, ever, and shout in front of my wife or my friend; I will break your fucking neck. Understood?'

The heavy half-heartedly tried to open the gate; he did not really want access to the yard or Peter.

Peter screamed 'Understood?'

Both visitors, Jessica and Cathy jumped in surprise. Landlord cowered, shrinking down the gate by six inches; he turned his face away and nodded.

'My friends in environmental health may just visit your restaurant. Or they may not. Now goodbye Landlord, off you trot.'

Peter opened the gate and watched the two visitors leave. As he turned, Jessica saw his flushed face and taut neck, but his gentle smile was genuine and his blue eyes twinkled, friendly.

'Rag Heads, don't they know they are guests in my city?'

This being the only occasion in Jessica's adult life, which she did not challenge a casual-racist remark. Cathy was not frightened of her husband, who was always gentle and protective, but she looked down at her hands giving him time to work out the adrenaline.

In *forces-speak*, Jessica's father called men like Peter - Pompey geezers, Plastic Cockneys. He was the salt of the earth. Hard but fair (unless you support Southampton Football Club, then he was just hard), friendly but suspicious. The Portsmouth island of Portsea had as many forts facing out against the rest of England, as it had sea forts facing out against the continent. For generations and centuries, Portsmouth had hosted and fought the Royal Navy, sending its sons to sea to die. This was a warrior city, a garrison town. Jessica with her olive skin, dark eyes and black hair, felt most welcome in Portsmouth but she knew she would only ever be a guest. She was one-eighth Afghan on her father's side and it showed pleasantly – she was attractive and sociable, but she was not a Pompey girl.

Now, the three adults sipped tea as April suckled.

'So Cath, you are basically a Friesian now?'

'Don't Jess. That is so true. I am nursing every three hours for twenty minutes. She is insatiable. And I swear she has teeth. I'm a sore milkshake machine.' Cathy wore a grin, but there was little humour in her voice. Tears welled in her eyes.

'Shit Cath, I was joking, so sorry. You are beautiful, fantastic.' Jessica leant to hug her friend, but Cathy eased the baby from her breast and handed her to Jessica to hold and wind.

Peter and Cathy laughed together, but the tears still streamed down her cheeks.

'Don't worry, Jess. Cath cries, sleeps, feeds, cries… you get the picture.'

'I don't just cry, I leak. I leak out my eyes, I leak out my chest, I even leak down my fucking legs.'

'Don't swear in front of April, love.'

If looks could kill, Pompey Geezer would be on the ground in a pool of blood. Cathy kept tugging on the right side of her shirt, with her left breast and red-raw nipple still exposed to the cool spring air. April began to cry and pulled her legs towards her chest; Jessica tried to wind her and failed. Panicking slightly she offered to hand baby back to mum but Cathy was not accepting.

'Don't give her to me, Jess. I can't wind her either, only superman here can.'

Still laughing, Peter scooped his baby from Jessica's chest with one hand. Jessica had not previously noticed how big Peter's hands were until she saw them against her own body. He lay the baby horizontal and brought her up to his shoulder in a gentle arch. Like a teddy bear being growled, April gave a long belch and stopped crying, Peter nuzzled her tummy through the blanket and placed her into the carrycot, asleep.

Cathy still tugged at the wrong side of her shirt. Jessica picked up the baby's muslin and gently patted dried milk from Cathy. She flinched with soreness; Jessica gently eased her back into her bra, buttoned her shirt, zipped her puffer jacket and gave her a long hug.

Wiping her eyes, Cathy apologised.

'So, lost your job, scrapping with lover-boy and pissed off Landlord. How do you stay so calm?'

'Pissed of Landlord?'

Peter spoke. 'He has been around knocking on your door. He had his key in hand, but I stood watching and he decided not to let himself in.'

'Thanks, Pete. I need to sort out some stuff. I owe him a month's rent for a start.'

'Yeah, well. This time next month he might have to go back home.'

'Sorry Pete, you lost me there.'

'He's talking Brexit Jess, ignore him. Peter is the only person in the country to think we will actually vote *leave* next month.'

'So Pete, Landlord is from Bangladesh, not really in the EU, is it? Why would he have to "go back home" and anyway his home is Fratton, four miles from here?'

'Yeah, that's right Jess. Stick up for him. You lot always stick together.'

Jessica's jaw tightened and she sat upright to face Peter. Before she could speak, Cathy intervened.

'Peter! Don't be so rude. Apologise, like now!'

Again, Jessica made to speak but Cathy held up a hand. 'Pete!'

'Sorry, Jess. I really am. He just irritates me.' Peter gave Jessica his best cheeky-chav smile, but Jessica and Cathy continued to glare at him. 'Honestly, I am sorry. All you lot, from Norfolk, look the same to me.'

Jessica threw a cushion at him. She felt irritated by this conversation, but Peter and the entire city were unlikely to change overnight.

'I've been *shatting* myself about the whole Zika Virus thing, with little princess here just being born. The sooner we pull up the drawbridge, the better.'

'Zika virus is in Brazil Pete! Do you honestly think that a virus from the other side of the world could ever possibly affect us here, in the U.K.?'

'I've explained all this to him, Jess. He is convinced the entire country will have to lockdown because of some foreign virus and that we are going to leave the EU – ridiculous. He's a naïve Pompey nutter!'

'Ok ladies, I am sat just here. Anyway, I have placed £250 on a three-way accumulator at the bookies. Within five years Trump will be president of the USA, the U.K. will have locked down against a viral pandemic and we have left the EU. Think of it as a long-term investment.'

'Yes darling, and we have £250 to throw away now, what with a new baby and everything.'

A throat cleared by the open gate. Landlord stepped awkwardly into the yard and stood looking towards Peter but without making eye contact.

'Miss Khan. We need to talk. Really, right now.'

Back in the tiny kitchen, Landlord declined a seat and stood respectfully by the open front door as Jessica poured him water from the fridge and started the coffee machine for herself.

'Before you say anything Landlord, I am sorry I have missed a payment. I will transfer the money today, pay a month in advance and sort out my banking order. And I promise I will sign the new contract this week and get it back to you.' Jessica waived the envelope from the top of the breadbin for emphasis. 'Sorry I have messed you around. It has been hectic.'

'Three months, Miss Khan.'

'Sorry?'

'You have missed three months of rent. That isn't a contract in the envelope that is an eviction notice.'

'No. What, really? Three months? No. Really?'

'Really.'

'Shit. Ok, no problem. Walk with me to the ATM, I will withdraw as much cash as I am allowed and transfer the rest immediately. Three months, really?'

'Sorry, Miss Khan. It is way too late for all that. You are evicted with immediate effect. If you pay the arrears, I will withdraw the County Court Judgement application – and even that will cost me. But I have new tenants waiting to move in. I won't need to clean or decorate…' Landlord scanned the perfectly maintained décor '… so I can give you until Thursday. One week. Then you must be out. My new family move in on the Friday.'

'Family? In this cupboard!'

Landlord shrugged.

Jessica sat on *the* tiny sofa, not really *her* tiny sofa anymore, with the new notebook open at the list page. She titled the page '2016 – The Start Of My New Life' and added more entries to the left-hand column of headers. She also completed some action points against the original headers. As the light faded, her list now read:

2016 - The Start Of My New Life
1. Work ✓ *- Finished at the Company. Take a long break and then find something I love to do; helping people or looking after animals. Rabbits or Blind Dogs.*
2. Chris ✓ *- Moved on from Chris. Take back control of my life. Make my own decisions. Don't lean on Amara, now that Chris has gone.*
3. Flat ✓ *- Moved on. Buy or rent bigger, or maybe ask Landlord for my tiny flat back if new tenants cannot squeeze in.*

4. *Travel Europe   A Road Trip. Thelma And Louise. (Or just Thelma).*
5. *Make awesome new friends*
6. *Wild Camp*
7. *Meet a rich, handsome, guy*
8. *Stay in the poshest ever boutique hotel and pamper myself*
9. *Swim in a waterfall*
10. *Just Live A Little*
11. *Prioritise myself*
12. *Wear a soldier's uniform and fire his gun*

Jessica poured another Pinot, chilling nicely and not intending to drink too much. She thought of Chris; walking to her bedroom window to see if the American marines were in the bar opposite.

That boat has sailed

She was not sure if she thought the boat had sailed with the marines, Chris, her past life, or with just her onboard alone.

Jessica used the landline to phone her sister. She needed to buy a personal mobile as soon as possible. Chris was tech-savvy and she would previously have taken his advice.

'Hey, Sissy! How's it going? Just catching-up.'

'Goodness, is that you, Jessica? It's been so long since you called last, what do you need?'

'Easy with the passive-aggression Sis, I have never needed anything from you. I was thinking of popping over tomorrow and updating you. I have made a few changes to my life and thought you might be interested.'

'What, actual changes or just a new list?'

'Changes. And a bit of a... Look, just forget it!'

'Hey Jess, don't get bolshie. Come over. Come to tea. You could do with some proper food and fattening up a bit.'

'Christ Sis! I eat fine and I have put the weight back on, since Richard. What is up with you?'

'Calm down, Jess. It has been such a long time since you visited...'

'Enough! I will drop-in at four, see the kids, say hello, swallow anything you try to force-feed me and then see mum and dad.'

'That will be lovely, Jess. Dad will be pleased to see you, after so long.'

'It hasn't been long! And what, mum does not want to see me, is that what you are getting at?'

'I never said that Jess, not exactly.'

Jessica slammed down the phone, ending the call.

Jessica did not hear the doorbell but her friend's voice over the intercom woke her, the flat dark.

'Hey Vanilla! Let me in. Or are you busy bonking stallion muffin? You there Chris, short for Christopher?'

Jessica smiled to herself, flicked the light and pushed the outer-door release. Opening the flat door, Jessica watched her friend climb the stairs, trying not to sway.

Jessica moved to give Amara a peck on the lips but received a slightly longer kiss than expected, before Amara slid past and into the flat.

'Hey, birthday girl! No man in the flat?'

'No Am, no man, no flat.'

Jessica seldom saw Amara tipsy and giggled as Amara blinked slowly in concentration.

'It is over between Chris and me and I have been evicted for not paying my rent.'

Amara sat heavily onto the arm of the sofa. 'You finished with him? How did he take it?'

'He didn't *take* anything, he *gave* it. He finished with me. I have been a prize arse recently; I guess he just had enough. He'll be rodgering one of the librarians or grads by the end of the week – more his type, anyway. Less *flighty*, perhaps.'

'And lost the flat, Jess? You love this flat!'

'I love Chris as well, Amara. Not to worry.'

Jessica shrugged. Amara felt Jessica's eyes were less accepting of the situation than her comment suggested. Amara moved to hug her friend but Jessica turned away and took the two steps needed to reach the Pinot fridge.

'So what happens now, Vanilla? Where to start? Obviously, you can stay with me in Guildford.'

'I'm still writing my list...' Jessica shot a brief glance at Amara. Amara and Chris seemed to be her only people who did not scoff or react to her journal and list writing. '... but so far it looks like

42

I am going to spend a lump of my redundancy on a massive road trip around Europe, perhaps a year. Along the way I am going to find myself the hottest sugar daddy, seduce his even hotter son, or daughter,…' Jessica grinned at Amara '… and then buy myself a vegan rabbit farm, before settling down back in Norfolk and having 2.4 babies with the most exciting and gorgeous fighter pilot you have ever seen. He'll wear his flying fatigues down the aisle; you know how I love a uniform.'

Jessica's speaking sped up; Amara saw her trying hard not to cry, and it almost worked. She interrupted Jessica's flow. She wanted to ask about the vegan rabbit farm, but instead she asked about the trip around Europe.

'Like, on your own Jess? You sure you will be comfortable on your own? It's a big world out there.' Amara saw Jessica's expression harden but before she could clarify, Jessica replied.

'Yeah Am, that's it. I can't do anything in life unless Christopher or Amara is holding my hand!' Amara did not respond. She gave her friend the room to fume for a moment.

'And more importantly, Jess – what exactly is a vegan rabbit farm?' Jessica's shoulders dropped a little as she relaxed. Both women took a deep gulp of wine. 'So, let's check this list.'

Amara sat on the sofa seat and straightened the Watch Log on the coffee table. Jessica reached to take the notebook; she did not like people looking at her journal or lists. Amara laid a restraining left hand across the opposite empty page. Her fingers long and slim, her nails wore an opaque gel-red varnish and her dark skin looked like a henna tattoo across the white page. Jessica was easily distracted by this woman's looks and elegance, all she managed today was to lay her own hand over her friend's.

Absentmindedly, Amara corrected punctuation and then added comments in her perfect handwriting.

Lubricated with wine and fuelled on nibbles and a shared bowl of noodles from the local takeaway, the friends talked of everything and nothing through the late evening – updating the list as new ideas sprang to mind. The occasional bursts of giggles and coarse language should have been a warning to Jessica that the list would need to be started again tomorrow, but at the time it all made sense to her.

Late into the early hours of Thursday morning, Amara called a taxi for the brief journey to her hotel and left Jessica to climb into bed.

Jessica spent the day cancelling bank orders and closing utility accounts, buying a new mobile phone with free European Roaming and packing her household possessions into sturdy plastic crates from the local Staples stationary superstore. She bathed, applied a tiny amount of makeup around her eyes, lipstick, dressed in fake-designer skinny jeans that a friend had brought back from a Turkish holiday and slipped into a skimpy top, which she knew her sister would hate her wearing in front of her husband.

She hugged her nieces and sat on the floor, talking boy-bands and clothes for the half-hour before supper. Her sister piled overcooked vegetables on top of a nicely braised steak in red wine sauce, so that she could visibly angst as Jessica picked her way through the vegetables to find the meat.

'Oh darling, if only you could eat better. Can't you just try?'

'So girls, Aunty Jess is going on an adventure – how exciting?'

Feeling like a child talking to a teddy bear in the Abuse Suite of a police station, knowing that the grown-ups were listening, Jessica continued.

'And, I will FaceTime you from every country I visit. I am going to live in my car…'

'But aunty, your car hasn't got a roof!'

'It has sometimes, darling, don't worry. And I am going to have lots of adventures and marry a prince. I will be just like Shirley Valentine in the DVD you gave me. '

'But prettier!' Shouted the eldest.

After pudding, an Eton Mess Jessica brought with her, the girls left the adults at the table. Jessica's brother-in-law reached across and squeezed her hand. His wife visibly tensed.

'Good for you, Jess. Well done. Most of the women we know, of your age, have dropped a sprog or two and slipped into suburbia. You are a brave kid.'

His wife sniffed loudly, scraped and banged together the plates, making sure she stretched between the two to force them apart. As she quickly sat down again, she grabbed both her husband's hands.

'Thanks Bro. You've probably guessed Chris and I have split. I took a work sabbatical, and the flat is too tiny to stay in for another year,' Jessica lied 'and so I decided it was time to live a little.'

'But what about money, darling? Now you haven't got Christopher to support you?'

'I have plenty of fucking money, Sis!' The girls giggled from the next room. Jessica lowered her voice and looked at her brother-in-law. 'Sorry, Bro.'

Brother-in-law laughed and ruffled Jessica's hair, probably the only man alive who would get away with it.

'They've heard worse, Jess. Your sister here spent two days screaming at me when I insisted we didn't have enough money for her boob job and a holiday.'

'What is the point of me going through all of that pain, just for you, if you didn't take me somewhere hot to show them off?' shrieked Jessica's sister.

Jessica and her brother-in-law gave each other a sideways glance before snorting into laughter. The girls, hearing their mother shriek and their father laugh, joined in with the giggling. Sister refused to storm-out and leave her husband alone with her sibling.

'Sis, I earn more than Chris, have less outgoings and commitments than he does and hugely more disposable income. I am my own woman.' Jessica held her sister's glare.

'And she doesn't need to spend money on a boob job either by the look of it, love.'

He went to ruffle his wife's hair and was batted away.

'But darling, we just worry about you. And I will miss you for a whole year. When do you go?'

Peter moved Jessica's plastic crates into the yard and used a tarpaulin to protect them until Amara had passed a message to Chris to collect and store them in his garage. Jessica hoped he might have met her to say goodbye, but he did not. There was no furniture, as the flat was let furnished.

Jessica's sister- and brother-in-law visited during the week. With Jessica's parents and input from an expert extreme-camping friend, they bought Jessica a top of the range waterproof backpack, with a built-in solar-powered light and device charger and a secure wired pocket with tether for security. A soft, partly inflatable bedroll – Bro insisted on buying a double for when Jessica got lucky, much to the disgust of her mother and sister and the amusement of her father – and a super-lightweight two-man hiking tent. Sis also bought Jessica a book. Jessica studied the cover and turned it over, reading the blurb.

'Thanks Sis. I love the cover art, an eye within an eye – looks a bit paranormal. Rapid Eye Movement by Amanda Sheridan, I have heard of her.'

'You take everything I say the wrong way Jessica, but I just thought it might keep you company if you feel lonely.' Jessica gave her the benefit of the passive-aggressive doubt, but she had no intention of feeling or being lonely. 'It's about these two women who are in each other's dreams and despite everything, they become ever closer. It isn't, let's say, always easy for them.'

Inside the front cover, Sis had written *Blood runs thicker than water.* Sis had not addressed or signed the note, but it oozed emotion for Jessica.

Jessica stood to hug her sister, but did not know how. Awkwardly, the two stood slightly apart before Bro stepped forward and clamped them together in a three-way bear hug.

With everything packed into her tiny Mazda MX5 two-seater sports car and the car parked securely in the neighbour's garage for one night, Jessica took her notebook and began the new volume of her journal. She speed-read the mess of her list covered in notes, scribbles and rude cartoons that she and Amara composed on the previous Wednesday, and shook her head at her own irreverence – her journals normally sacred to her. Carefully, she pulled the page away from the perforated margin and slid it away, across the coffee table. She wrote just a few lines in her journal, before starting the Amanda Sheridan novel – a few pages would be enough to relax her ready for bed. She glanced at her list again, before folding it several times into a bookmark for REM. The list had become more bizarre as that night had progressed. It now read:

2016 - The Start Of My New Life
1. Work ✓ - Finished at the Company. Take a long break and then find something I love to do; helping people or looking after animals. Rabbits or Blind Dogs.

2. Chris ✓ - Moved on from Chris. Take back control of my life. Make my own decisions. Don't lean on Amara, now that Chris has gone. Lean on me as much as you want, my love!

3. Flat ✓ - Moved on. Buy or rent bigger, or maybe ask Landlord for my tiny flat back if new tenants cannot squeeze in.

4. Travel Europe A Road Trip. Thelma And Louise. (Or just Thelma). And beyond Europe.

5. Make awesome new friends for life

6. Wild Camp And go wild

7. Meet a rich, handsome, guy your own age! Maybe more mature Fall in love Or lust!

8. Stay in the poshest ever boutique hotel and pamper myself and buy a holiday home ~ aim for the stars

9. Swim in a waterfall and be dried by the sun or a hunk

10. Just Live A Little and stay safe Or at least stay alive

11. Prioritise myself over and above anyone else - you are the most important

12. Wear a soldier's uniform and fire his gun kinky! fight him for it first

13. Fall back into your friend's arms - I will always be ready to catch you

Peter and Cathy sat in the backyard with April devouring her mother as usual; waiting for Jessica to appear. Peter accepted the flat key and slid it into his pocket before the party escorted Jessica to her car, now parked ready on the neighbour's drive. Landlord leant against the drive gate. He stepped awkwardly towards Jessica and gave her a firm man-hug, making little body contact except for the very tip of his shoulder against her chest, and his forearms on her back. 'Good luck, Miss Khan. Please return safely to your friends.'

Jessica climbed into the driver's seat and folded down the soft-top. She gave a stifled scream of surprise when she first saw Amara in the passenger seat, wearing a huge grin. They briefly hugged, Amara saving the proper hugs and kisses until they were alone. Jessica slipped the car into gear and waved out of the open roof as the two friends made the brief journey through the city to the Continental Ferry Port. Perhaps for the first time in their close relationship, it was Amara who cried and could not stop kissing and hugging Jessica, as they said their goodbyes.

Once boarded, Jessica made for the viewing deck and looked back towards the city, as the ferry juddered into Portsmouth Harbour.

None of her family came to wave goodbye, and Chris was most conspicuous by his absence. However, Amara stood on the dock waving frantically. As the ferry turned almost out of sight, Jessica watched Amara barge two burly dockies out of the way to maintain the line of sight. As Jessica waved back, her brightly coloured floppy bucket sunhat caught the change in wind direction and floated towards the railings and freedom.

'Madam, yours, I think? It is a most unusual design – like an artist's palette.'

An older man, perhaps mid-sixties, strode towards Jessica, his arm outstretched and holding her hat.

'HowzHat! Well caught, sir!'

Jessica's cricket reference and play on words were lost on this foreign gentleman, but he returned a sweet, if slightly bemused, smile. As Jessica made to take the hat, the man grasped it gently in both hands, setting it squarely on Jessica's head. Not at the jaunty angle she would normally wear it, but

53

smoothly done. He brushed hairs from her forehead and offered her a pressed white handkerchief. Jessica smiled, tilted her head and frowned, not only at the offer of a handkerchief but also at the completely unsolicited and quite intimate contact.

'Please forgive me. I noticed your farewell tears. I hope they are tears of happiness.'

Jessica was about to answer, before deciding not to explain herself to this stranger. This really quite attractive, perfectly groomed stranger with hazel eyes flecked with green and smelling of lemon cologne. She ignored the handkerchief and wiped the back of her hand across her eyes and nose. Then, touching her face to check she had not wiped snot across it, she grabbed the handkerchief, dabbing her cheek.

'I almost lost my hat on the maiden voyage. Thank you. Perhaps I can buy you and your wife a coffee?'

Why did I mention wife?

'That will be most kind. This is a French boat; perhaps the coffee is… acceptable.'

They sat together, and there was no wife, at least not on this boat. They talked throughout the journey – mostly about Jessica, her recent challenges, and her new adventure. He introduced himself as Albay Salepci, but Jessica came away with little other information. She enjoyed this man's company. His humour a gentle mix of the polite, with a little risqué, reminding her of the officer humour she encountered at home as a teenager and when working for the Company, dealing with the Royal Navy. The encounter kept her mood light; at a time she may easily have slipped into melancholy. Moreover, he was charming and quite easy on the eye. Jessica carefully avoided flirting overly and so embarrassing this man, easily twice her age, but she certainly felt relaxed in his company. He gracefully allowed Jessica to pay for the coffees and Danish.

She offered him her mobile number, but not yet knowing it off by heart, swiped open the new phone. Talking about her planned route, Albay took her phone and placing it next to his, tapped the two screens until both phones bleeped receipt of a message. He handed back the phone, apologising for having powered down by mistake.

As the tannoy called for foot passengers to disembark in France, Jessica offered to drive her new friend to the station, but he declined. He moved to kiss Jessica on both cheeks and she clinched a long embrace. Albay removed a pendant wrapped in tissue paper from his jacket pocket; a heavy glass teardrop hanging from a leather lace, in circular shades of blues, greens and turquoise and a dark round 'eye' off-centre on a white swirl.

'For you, my sweetheart. Maybe a necklace, or perhaps to hang in your car. It is Nazar Boncuk, an eye to deflect the evil eye. A good luck charm for your journey, for your adventure. And who knows, it may bring you back to me, in Athens perhaps.'

Jessica lowered the roof on her car again and drove off the ferry just as the continental sun set. The evil eye swayed gently from the rear-view mirror.

Jessica spent the first week of her adventure driving south through France. Not holding herself to any routine, she removed her watch and silenced the alarm on her phone. She quickly settled into living from a backpack. She listened to a podcast interview of a travel memoir author having lived only on white rice, to help stretch her travel finances. With Jessica's redundancy package in the bank, she felt able to live some days quite frugally and splash out on others. She enjoyed both.

Jessica visited Paris, arriving late and sleeping in her car parked on a back road in the 8th arrondissement. Woken by the increasing traffic, she sat in the passenger seat and wriggled out of her designer gingham *driving* dungarees that Chris had bought for a previous birthday beach-party and into a deep blue, silky summer gala dress over white leggings and a white cotton camisole. With only a couple of embarrassing moments with passersby, she was soon dressed and ready to join the early morning crowds on the Champs-Élysées, just a short walk away. She purchased a ticket for the Louvre on her new iPhone, bypassing the growing queue. Elbowing past a coach of South Koreans, Jessica had most of the galleries to herself – following behind the swathe of tourists ahead and protected by the impenetrable wall of Coach Koreans, grazing slowly behind.

She reached the barrier around Leonardo da Vinci's The Mona Lisa and found herself stood in awe. The painting was much smaller than she imagined, but the image was the most mesmerising and beautiful she had seen. The assistant curator caught her eye and smiled.

'She is the most beautiful, no?' Her English was perfect, heavily accented. 'Your first time?' Jessica nodded dumbly.

The curator began a well-rehearsed speech, explaining a little of the mystique surrounding the most famous smile in the world. The Koreans caught-up and formed a scrum around Jessica, their strange exclamations drowning out the velvet voice of the curator. One member of the party forced her way in front of Jessica and shouted a conversation to the man who stood, too closely, behind Jessica. With no foreknowledge of what she was about to do, Jessica heard herself scream out.

'Shut up, quiet! Shut the fuck-up and... just, queue!'

Before the words had completely left her mouth, two security guards gripped her wrists, and the curator made herself into a shield between Jessica and the painting from behind the rope barrier. The guard spoke in French as the curator translated for Jessica.

'Keep your hands by your sides and move to your right.' Spoken in fluent velvet.

The coach party videoed and snapped photographs of the unfolding scene. The man who had been pushing against her back spun around to take a selfie of himself, with Jessica being *restrained* in the background.

Facing a wall some distance away, Velvet spoke to the guards who smiled at Jessica and walked away. The two women looked at each other for a moment, before bursting into spontaneous laughter. Jessica apologised for her inappropriate behaviour and Velvet said how much she had wanted to do the same so often. As they talked, Jessica explained which hotel she was staying in, or at least, which one she had parked outside and Velvet recommended a steak restaurant around the corner. Jessica continued her tour through the museum and toward the exit. As she passed, each staff-member brought a radio to their face, to report her progress.

Jessica continued her walking trip around the tourist attractions, visited the Eiffel Tower and caught an afternoon matinee at the Moulin Rouge. The show was high adrenalin, with beautiful, bare-chested dancers, incredibly risky acrobatics and even circus horses on stage. At one point, a glamorous mermaid swam with live sharks in a glass tank as dancers performed scenes from Hans Christian Anderson's The Little Mermaid. The closing scene comprised the most beautiful ballet-style dance. A young dancer, wearing only a fine and transparent body stocking, presumably because of her young years, posed in a frame and was being *painted* by a young God-of-a-man, wearing only a few smudges of his artist's paints for modesty. As he *created* his canvas, the girl grew more animated until he pulled her from the frame and the two danced the most romantic of love scenes. As the final curtain lowered, the audience exploded into applause and tears streamed down Jessica's cheeks.

Back at the car, she wriggled out of her leggings and discretely removed the camisole as late evening commuters streamed past. She changed her Sketchers for golden sandals and unknotted the silk scarf she wore around her waist, draping it over her shoulders to take the eye away from her plunging neckline.

All eyes turned to Jessica as she entered the Steak Restaurant and she felt grown-up and desirable; the bohemian, independent, young female traveller that she was. Perhaps she should have applied a second puff of perfume, to mask the busy 48 hours since her last shower – a French Bath. As she was shown to a table for one, Velvet from the Louvre took her hand and speaking to the maitre d', pulled Jessica to her own table.

'I said to my husband that you might eat here.'

Velvet introduced Jessica to a tall slim man of her own age and the three sat together.

'I recommend the steak au poivre.' His voice was silk.

Velvet has married Silk.

Silk ordered the food and wine, as Velvet explained they had decided to drink and gossip together for a while, waiting to see if Jessica came to the restaurant, before ordering. They both occasionally talked to the neighbouring table. The clientele spoke mostly English within Jessica's earshot and conversation centred on the recent heavy-handed anti-terror police operations. Velvet lightened the conversation.

'Ok Jessica. Our friends want to hear exactly how you organised our visitors today.'

'No! You are embarrassing me, stop it Velvet.'

Silk added, 'You are our English celebrity. You are famous, at least in this corner of the restaurant.'

Jessica took a long drink of wine, before laughing nervously. The restaurant grew quiet and several tables turned to look.

'This is so embarrassing. Look, all I said was...' Jessica exaggerated her best cockney/Portsmouth accent and as loudly as she felt appropriate, shouted 'This is Leonardo da Vinci's Mona fucking Lisa, not some K-pop poster! Now shut the fuck up, show some respect and form a *putain de file*!'

Jessica's audience laughed and clapped before returning to their meals and her table returned to the steaks, sniggering. Once the couple realised Jessica intended sleeping in her car, they insisted she stay with them. The three spent the rest of the evening drinking, laughing, and talking about Jessica's travel plans and art. Jessica felt surprised with how at ease she felt discussing art with these two experts – they reminded her of the 'awesome new friends' entry on her discredited list. If she still had that scrap of paper she would add another tick, before finally consigning it to the bin.

Back at their small and draughty flat, Silk pulled apart the two four-foots that formed their own bed and insisted Jessica have one, whilst the couple shared the other. Jessica fell asleep to the hum of traffic around the Arc de Triomphe and dreamt of her ferryboat friend, Albay. He was watching her sleep through a turquoise, circular patterned window; in her dream, she did not mind him spying on her.

She woke late in the morning; her new friends had left for work. Jessica read a note inviting her to use the small sit-up baignoire, and croissants with a flask of fresh coffee sat on the bedside cabinet. She wondered if they would notice her still being there in the evening.

Not staying, but continuing through France, Jessica spent several nights wild camping, sleeping in her car or staying in bed-and-breakfast; visiting medieval towns, museums and even churches – any venue enabling her to talk with people as well as to see something interesting or learn something new. Heading east, she drove over the Alps to Italy, blasting through the tunnels and over bridges and viaducts with the roof folded down. She wore a huge grin as she took the racing line on mountain roads – feeling like Sophia Loren in a sixties movie or perhaps a bond girl. Bored children, sat on the backseats of family cars, lorry drivers and handsome Italian men, returned her smiles – latterly, often followed by a slap on the arm from a female passenger.

Once in Tuscany she wound her way through the countryside, visiting tiny hilltop villages and vineyards, camping on the grounds or at the side of the road each night - on one occasion listening to wild boar rummaging around her camp. She enjoyed every moment, the times of isolation and the moments with company. Jessica often thought of Chris but did not regret completing this journey alone, not that Chris had given her a choice.

Parking in a supermarket car park, Jessica washed and dried clothes in a coin-operated mini-laundrette, packed her backpack and caught a train to Riomaggiore, the furthest east of the beautiful Cinque Terre villages. She spent the day exploring the tiny cobbled streets with the other day-tourists, before finding an expensive room above an art shop in the main street. With the peeling pastel chocolate-box houses and shops glowing in the evening sun, she made her way down the cobbled street to the tiny harbour, little more than a slipway, and an almost empty seafood café. Catch of the Day was the only menu choice. Jessica chose Catch of the Day.

A fit, good-looking Englishman in his late thirties with a mop of fair hair and quite chiselled features, moved from his table to sit on the restaurant wall and argue into his mobile.

'No Kris, I said Riomaggiore. You are at completely the wrong end.

'No, do what you want, I will find a room here and start hiking west tomorrow – we can meet in the middle, or you can hop on the train and meet up in Manarola. Keep in touch. Is the room in Kris Taylor, or Jason Taylor?'

Jessica missed the end of the conversation as the man walked a few steps along the slipway.

Back in the café, he signalled for a beer and sat back at his table, giving Jessica a smile and nod.

'Hi, Jason Taylor.'

'Hey, Jessica Khan.'

They shook hands and Jessica held him a moment longer than necessary.

'Do you want to split a meal, Jessica? They only serve a whole fish here and there is enough to feed a family!'

The couple pulled together the two single tables. They shared a carafe of white wine with the fish and then a carafe of red wine with the gelato, which the waiter brought them from a neighbouring shop. They shared each other's ice cream. Feeling a warm glow from the fresh air and wine - Jessica was in a sharing mood.

'Where are you staying? Did I hear a mix-up with the room, with your... partner.'

'Ah Jessica, man. He's an *effing* nightmare; I don't know why we try to go on holiday together; I should leave the prick at home.'

'Because you love him, perhaps? Please call me Jess.'

'Ha! Yes. I do love him, Jess, but that doesn't stop him from being a prick. I'll ask the manager here where to find a room.'

Jessica pushed the melting bubblegum flavoured ice cream around her bowl for a moment, chewing her bottom lip.

'Look Jason, I fully understand if you say no, of course I would, but I've ended up with a big twin *that's a shame* room tonight if you want to share me? I mean, you share me – share the room with me, I mean.'

'Sure Jess, great idea. Thanks. And call me Jace, only Kris and mum call me Jason.'

They walked around the harbour and small-town after dinner. Occasionally Jason took her hand to hold her attention and on a slippery section of cobbles, she slipped her arm through his. Back at the room, Jason arranged his bed for the night and discretely changed into fresh boxer shorts whilst sat on the bed with a towel over his lap. He showered, before drying in the cramped shower room and then wore the towel over his boxers to walk back to the bed, climbing under the sheets and tossing the towel over a chair.

'I will have to leave the door open if ok, Jace? I'm a bit claustrophobic.' Jessica lied.

Jessica spent some time drying her hair, looking into the bathroom mirror, her naked back exposed to Jason. Once she had taken as long as possible to complete this task, she slowly dried her entire body and moisturised, before reaching for the smallest dry towel and wrapping it around her waist – walking back into the bedroom topless. Jason lay on his back, facing slightly away and snoring lightly.

Man! You are kidding me!

Jessica flopped down hard onto her own bed, throwing the towel over her sleeping companion.

Jessica woke to an empty room; Jason's rucksack sat on the chair and his bedding pulled down neatly. Walking into the bright morning sun, Jessica found Jason sipping an espresso with the Art Shop assistant. She had a cappuccino.

'Morning, Tess! Thought we'd grab some breakfast and maybe start the hike together? See how we get on, you know, pace-wise.'

Jessica nodded and walked up the street towards a row of cafés and gelato shops. Cappuccino girl stepped back to avoid Jessica walking into her and blushed deeply. Jason caught up within a couple of strides and Cappuccino heard Jessica snap at her friend, but could not quite catch the English words.

'Jess, Jason. My name is Jess, not Tess!'

'Yeah, I know Jess. I know that.'

Jessica took a deep breath. 'Pretty girl, if you like that sort of thing. All big eyes and little tits.'

'Yeah Jess, tell me about it, she is lovely! And most obliging.'

Jessica stopped and glared at Jason.

'What? I told her we were hiking the Cinque Terre, and she gave me some information maps and a coffee.'

'Whatever, gay boy.' Jessica continued to a café.

The couple walked the ancient route between villages, diverting to secluded coves and beaches to swim and share Jessica's snorkel and mask; sitting on Jessica's bedroll on an empty pebble beach to eat lunch and dry off in the sun. She wore the more modest and practical of her two bikini bottoms, and he wore yesterday's boxer shorts to swim – not having come prepared. Jessica mentioned the early morning conversation.

'Look, Jace, I really am sorry about first thing. I went to bed in a foul mood.'

'Lost me there, Jess. I thought you were a bit quiet, but nothing to apologise for.'

 Jessica smiled. 'I'm single at the moment and I was hoping, you know.'

'Yeah, same here. I'm single. What were you hoping for?'

'You're married to Kris! One argument about a hotel reservation hardly makes you single.'

Jason snorted, chuckled and then belly laughed; Jessica could not help but join in. Eventually, he spoke.

'So that's why you called me gay boy! Kris is my brother, not my husband! Oh, I see what you mean now, I see what you were hoping for last night.' Jason rolled on to his side towards Jessica, cupping her face with his hand. 'You should have said.'

By the time they were ready to leave the beach, it was too dark and dangerous to walk the narrow cliff path, so they camped out under the stars, splitting the remains of their picnic for supper and breakfast. Early the following morning they woke to a Park Ranger and as Jessica pulled her hiker sleeping bag across her naked body, Jason paid the eighty-euro fine for wild camping on the Cinque Terre.

They continued their hike, soaking up the breathtaking mountain and village views and

Mediterranean vistas, before arriving late at the only hostel along the route; the dormitories segregated. They believed Jessica was alone in the darkened female dorm but as Jason tried to sneak in, there was a loud throat-clear from a bunk in the opposite corner and Jason beat a silent retreat.

In the morning, Jessica arrived in reception to find a post-it note left with the desk. "Sorry Jess." Jessica noticed the J corrected from a T. "I've had to get the train back to Rioma to collect the prick." The note signed with a kiss, a smiley face and a mobile number.

Jessica slipped the post-it into her journal and continued the hike alone. Although she would have enjoyed a rematch with the slim and toned Jason, she was happy to have her own space back again. Remembering her ill-fated list, she had also wanted some holiday lust, not just love.

CHAPTER 7 – AWESOME NEW FRIENDS

Having completed the Cinque Terre alone, she collected the car and now snaked around The Lakes, spending one night camped on the edge of Lago D'Iseo. She spent the following late morning exploring Verona and staring at *that* balcony. An American, middle-aged female tourist spoke to Jessica, in a deep southern drawl.

'Isn't it just the most touching love story? And look how old everything is.' She shouted her question, in case Jessica could not speak English.

Jessica smiled and thought deeply before answering.

'Yes, most touching. A thirteen-year-old child groomed for sex, only to kill herself when her family and the authorities intervened. Most wholesome. I wonder if she played the banjo.' The tourist appeared shocked by Jessica's response and moved closer to her husband, asking if he knew Juliet had a banjo.

Continuing her journey, Jessica had a *splash-out* night and booked into the Terme di Sirmione Spa Hotel. After an hour exploring the quaint cobbled village on Lake Garda, she changed into her less modest La Perla bikini in swirly reds and orange.

Selecting a white compulsory swim hat, to contrast her olive skin and dark eyes, Jessica floated out across the hot-spring pools – swimming back to the edge only long enough to order the occasional Prosecco.

On one of her well-earned Prosecco breaks, Jessica introduced herself to a Belgian man named Belgi. He spoke softly in Pidgin English and his dark eyes twinkled; the new companions rested against the edge of the pool. Occasionally he would imitate a movie or television catchphrase in better spoken-English than he normally managed and with a perfectly colloquial British or American accent, making her laugh into her wine flute. After fifteen minutes of talking, a wet mop of blond hair, tucked into a red swim hat, surfaced between them and Netter, with a perfect smile, introduced herself to Jessica as 'Belgi's.' Netter did not need to explain exactly what of Belgi's she was, as her closeness to Jessica when she said it clarified her point. Her breath smelled of toothpaste. As Belgi floated on his back, feet on the edge of the pool, the two women talked and became instant friends. They agreed to eat together that evening in the hotel; with Belgi and Netter's (from Holland) Campervan parked outside the restricted-access village.

In true backpacker style and with less than a convinced expression from the pursed-lipped receptionist, Jessica ushered her new friends into her bedroom on the pretence of checking-it-out for their future stay and in turn, Netter smuggled a bottle of mini-market red wine. Despite having power-showered after the pools, the three felt almost as excited at soaking in the en-suite double whirlpool, as they did at being in this exclusive spa. Camping made people crave bathing, Jessica decided.

Belgi catnapped on the enormous bed, occasionally making duvet-angels against the Egyptian cotton, as Jessica soaked in the bath with plenty of bath oil and Netter reclined on the bathroom chaise lounge. She kept their glasses topped with the reasonable tasting and cheap Chianti, as they both discussed their pasts and futures. Netter was attentive and became more animated when Jessica talked about the string of bad luck with her job, flat and then Chris. At one point, she perched on the edge of the bath and massaged conditioner into Jessica's hair, as she explained about Chris.

Belgi and Netter planned to continue their camping trip as far as Istanbul in Turkey, where Netter intended to train the journey to Tehran in Iran, a trip she had wanted to do since a teenager.

Belgi would camp around the north and west of Turkey for a few days, before collecting Netter at Ankara, the capital of Turkey, or back at Istanbul. They had only met on this trip. All three were the same age, born within a few months of each other. Belgi worked for the family business and took long holidays each spring and Netter appeared the modern hippy – earning good money as a management consultant, but spending much of her time between contracts travelling. She was an obvious loner, much like Jessica. Lowering her voice, she told Jessica that she might phone Belgi from the train and call it off, either continuing east alone or back to Turkey and on to Europe by train.

Jessica dried her hair wearing the huge fluffy hotel dressing gown and applied a little make-up in the bathroom mirror, as the couple now soaked in the whirlpool. They then all dressed smart-casual, Jessica wore her Blue Gala Dress from her limited wardrobe, Netter wore a tiny sunset orange silk slip dress and Belgi wore loose stone linen trousers with a baby pink linen shirt; his boat shoes and belt buffed to hi-gloss on the hotel shoeshine machine. With a plunging neckline and split to the skirt of her dress, which hung mid-calf, Jessica smiled at her reflection.

The three made a striking thruple as they browsed the trinket shops in the village, Jessica buying slippers to match her dress, before heading back to the Spa Hotel and a long dinner on the terrace overlooking the hot spring pools and Lake Garda. The sky was clear, and the stars shone brightly in a moonless sky. Each table had an electric patio heater, and the three felt in no hurry for the evening to end. With the general bonhomie, the beautiful view and a little alcohol, Jessica saw Netter's eyes pool as the three eventually had to say goodnight and goodbye. Walking back towards their parked camper – Netter carried her heels and walking barefoot, leant against Belgi.

Jessica had an early morning full body massage, wax and a facial, before dressing in her loose trousers and wide striped navy-blue and white shirt. The belt had an exaggerated width and scrunched both the shirt and the trousers into calculated casualness. Although she was eating well, she had lost a little weight travelling and with the additional exercise her waist was now smaller and her stomach completely flat. She had to monitor her weight and eating habits, she could easily slip into being underweight again.

Jessica drove through Slovenia - camping by lakes, walking canyons and swimming in waterfalls. She stopped for supper in a tiny restaurant with two guest bedrooms; the second room occupied by a large German motorcyclist.

From the limited menu, Jessica ordered Slovenian Dumpling in a creamy chicken sauce. The German asked if he could perch on the end of her table and gently eased himself into the most accessible chair in the small dining area.

'What else you eat, madam?'

'No, that is all thanks. If I'm still hungry, I can always order a pudding.'

'Yes, ok. You eat some more now.'

The German with the sore hips laughed. 'She thinks you are too skinny to last a cold snap!'

Jessica preferred strangers not to comment on her, or anyone's, body image. However, she could see the funny side and smiled back.

'No really, that's all for now. I am fine.'

The young waiter shook her head, took Hips' order and disappeared into the kitchen. Shortly afterwards she returned with her mother; father peered around the corner. Mother spoke and daughter translated.

'Mati said, what you want lady?' Hips laughed again.

'Dumplings. That's all.'

With the Teutonic laughter as a soundtrack, Jessica was unsure if she found this bizarrely funny or just irritating – it was getting late. Mother lent forward, felt Jessica's forehead and pinched her cheeks, Jessica stifled a smirk. A few minutes later, Hips received his sausage starter and Jessica a plate of paste and a slice of toast. Before she could protest, the waiter left and Hips explained the father must have sent out a plate of lard – to keep her going until the dumplings arrived. Jessica managed half of the plate and to save her blushes, Hips had a large portion leaving just enough for politeness.

Hips explained that he had a fantastic trip booked in the Krizna Caves with a private guide. He had secured one of the few passes issued each year, but that he had hurt his hips on the mountain roads and would call to cancel in the morning – unless Jessica wanted to go in his place; Hips would accept no money for his ticket. He emailed Jessica his voucher and after sharing a small bottle of Krucefix schnapps and travelling stories, he then hobbled to bed. Jessica settled her own bill so that she could make an early start for the caves in the morning and picked up the tab for Hips meal and room - the whole bill less than forty pounds.

There was a slightly awkward moment at the cave entrance as she introduced herself as Hips and then tried to explain that she had forgotten how to speak German, lost around eight stone in weight and changed sex – as compared with Hips' medical declaration form. The guide eventually agreed to continue the expedition and took Jessica to explore around 2km of cave, including thirteen of the forty-five underwater lakes. There were no staff or office at the cave; the entrance in a secluded mountain pass with no mobile signal. Jessica was apprehensive - if either or both slipped or became ill, there would be no help arriving anytime soon. However, the guide appeared strong and confident, and Jessica's apprehension soon changed to excitement as they inched their way into the subterranean world. Jessica quickly fell into the rhythm of the guide, placing her own feet into the footsteps of the guide, to preserve the incredibly fragile and slow forming sinter.

Some lakes were shallow, looking like black mirrors, whilst others required rubber boats to cross. Dinghies were located along the route and from some lakes, the couple carried them over the rocks and sinter to access other lakes. The ambient darkness was absolute, but incredibly fifty species of animal lived in this alien world, including snails and translucent worms, cave hedgehogs and cave spiders. Many of the animals were naturally blind and indigenous to the cave system, or even to just part of the system.

The guide established Jessica was not scared of the absolute dark before turning out her lamp and carefully turning Jessica about face. Turning the lamp on again, she confronted Jessica with a huge rock formation nicknamed the iceberg, which loomed from the cavernous tunnel wall. The guide stood behind Jessica to catch her if she fell backward with vertigo. Then with the guide holding hands to steady her and turning off the lamp again, Jessica tried to spin around slowly so that she would face in the same direction – but so disorientated, she could not locate her original direction within the maze of tunnels, even with the lamps turned on again.

The final prank was for the guide to have Jessica sit at the front of the boat as she slowly paddled down a gently snaking subterranean river; admiring huge stalactites that loomed from the cave roof, which was far beyond the reaches of their head-torches. The guide having turned off the main lamp again asked Jessica to navigate around the stalagmites protruding from the riverbed, by head torch alone. As she paddled and Jessica navigated, she explained how the caves remained unexplored until just a few years ago, partly because of the folklore of dragons and demons. As they rounded a corner, Jessica felt a cold blast against her face and a low braying growl pierced the darkness just yards ahead. Unusually for Jessica, she screamed, scrambling down the boat to escape her assailant. The guide had moved forward to restrain Jessica and prevent her from injuring herself. With the guide laughing and soothing 'It's ok Hips, nothing is there' and Jessica whimpering, the two struggling women lay in the boat until the laughing of the guide had settled Jessica.

'What the fuck!'

Guide turned on the lamp and pointed to a split in the tunnel wall at water level. She explained that the bow-wave from their boat pushed water into the crevice, forcing air from a chimney and creating an air-horn effect.

Still trembling, Jessica joined in with nervous laughter, only playfully to punch the guide on the shoulder – much harder than appropriate. The guide flinched, grabbing her shoulder and laughing louder as she twisted away from Jessica in the bottom of the boat.

Finally, the two women pulled on to a subterranean beach and made a pot of tea using a gas primus stove and the naturally percolated lake water – caught on its journey to siphons and wells, before appearing in other cave systems and eventually surfacing at Lake Cerknica, and daylight.

In adversary or at least *in adrenalin*, Jessica made another lifelong friend. Guide refused a tip, and the two women swapped email addresses and mobile numbers.

Driving to Predjama Castle for her last night in Slovenia, Jessica pulled down the roof and eased along mountain roads. She turned the heater to full, with the pure mountain air gently tousling her hair. Negotiating a sharp bend at walking pace, she slammed the brakes to an emergency stop as a small mountain deer limped in front of the car. Almost immediately behind followed a brown bear crashing down the mountain slope and stopping halfway across the bonnet of her Mazda. The bear picked itself up and faced Jessica with a growl, standing to her full height. Steeled by her earlier encounter with a subterranean demon, Jessica put one hand on the horn, pushed the accelerator to the floor and so revving the engine, stood in the footwell of her tiny and now seemingly insignificant open car and screamed at the bear. Without a moment's hesitation, the bear dropped to all fours and slinked back onto the mountain slope.

Italy had been Jessica's favourite country, now it was Slovenia.

Jessica hugged the coast through Croatia and Montenegro. Stopping in Croatia for lunch, she began a conversation with a good-looking, rugged outdoor-type, who was making a delivery to the restaurant. It transpired he was the local truffle hunter, and the two walked with his manic dogs back into the forest surrounding the restaurant. The man explained, in English, how he hunted for the prized ingredient. He explained why they prefer dogs as they are less likely to eat the fungi than a pig. He trained them from birth, rubbing truffle onto the mother's teats to accustom the puppy to the smell. Jessica teamed with the slightly less manic dog and within forty minutes had wrestled a walnut-sized truffle from its jaws. The truffle was of inferior quality and the hunter offered she could keep it; a few days later she gently shaved it into a bottle of extra virgin olive oil for drizzling on to food – it was satisfyingly authentic, but a little bitter tasting.

Two days later, she arrived travel-exhausted to a glamping pod on the shore of Lake Shkoder, Albania. She spent the following days eating huge portions of freshwater fish and prawns with litres of beer, for the equivalent of less than ten pounds per day, including the accommodation.

On her last full day on Lake Shkoder, Jessica ferry hopped around the vast system of rivers and dams, ate freshwater crab with garlic soured cream served from port side stalls, and ferry-boated between huge fjord cliffs soaring out of the water. Returning to the campsite nine hours later and exhausted, she found Netter and Belgi had arrived in their camper and now sat around a fire pit with two dozen Albanian campers, teenagers to middle-aged. Jessica returned from the camp restaurant with an orange crate full of litre bottles of beer for the equivalent of eighty pence each. Many around the campfire thanked Jessica and helped themselves – the group then ensured the box never emptied.

Jessica picked-up a book by Pamdiana Jones called When In Roam, from the restaurant book swap.

'This is the woman I mentioned who ate white rice for months to help afford her travels. I think I might have eaten better than that and just gone home early!'

Jessica settled down between Netter and Belgi. Her legs across Belgi's and her head resting on

Netter's lap, her bottom sat on the oversized cushion that the couple shared. Netter absentmindedly toyed with Jessica's hair as Jessica flicked through When In Roam. She gently took the book from Jessica.

'No Jess, like this.' She held the book upside-down so that it opened on the most thumbed sections. 'You can always tell the best parts of an old book read by backpackers, they only thumb through the juicy sections!'

Jessica laughed and snatched the book back, now opened at one of the well-thumbed sections.

'My goodness Netter, you are only right, and good girl Pamdiana! Listen to this!' Jessica read out a section where the author had hooked-up with some friends on her travels.

'Jessica! We should so do this. You, me and Belgi. We could shower together, in the dark or candlelight and then, you know.'

'Netter! No way. Too much beer, young lady.' The Albanians could not follow the quick-fire conversation between the two women, even though they had not worried to lower their voices. Mostly in English with a smattering of French, a hybrid the women had casually developed, Belgi could catch the gist of what was being said and took a discrete interest. 'You would hate it in the morning. You would hate me, hate Belgi and hate yourself.'

'Like I so would not Jess.'

Netter pouted as she gently scratched Jessica's scalp through her hair. As she slipped her fingers down to tickle the back of her neck, Jessica jumped into the sitting position and playfully batted away Netter's hand.

'We could stay in your posh pod.'

Jessica laughed, partly at such the quintessentially English word 'posh' being dropped casually into a sentence with such a heavy Dutch accent. 'You are more than welcome to stay in my posh pod Netter, but nothing else. No!'

In a perfect Groucho Marx impersonation, whilst not understanding the meaning of all the words himself, Belgi added, 'Well ladies, I just love Posh Spice, but saffron is so expensive to buy.'

He accompanied the turn by pretending to smoke a huge cigar. The entire party laughed – Jessica because her being propositioned for sex had suddenly become part of a public spectacle, Netter with coyness, Belgi laughed at the reaction he had secured from the audience and the Albanians laughed at his impersonation. Nobody laughed at the joke.

The evening became more raucous. More beer purchased and then plastic bottles of wine appeared. The restaurant provided a plate of prawns cooked in garlic to share, free to encourage the alcohol sales. A teenager fetched a heavy plastic dog's ball with a bell inside, for a game of after-dark-catch. What started as a gentle passing of the ball, guided by the tinkle of the bell, quickly degenerated into a Roller Ball version, where the young men hurled the hardball at each other, and girls squealed when caught in the crossfire.

A couple of campers with young children asked the group to quieten down and the seemingly twelve-year-old night manager came to douse the fire. Jessica and Netter grabbed a half-bottle of wine to take back to the posh pod as Belgi tried to play the last few minutes of Roller Ball. He soon realised, at thirty years old, he was past-it and had become an easy target for the teenage lads. Holding his hands in surrender and waving goodnight to his adversaries, Belgi caught-up with the women at the pod.

He heard Jessica talking in a light voice. 'No Netter, no, no, no. N-O spells no. No! It might be fun, but still no. Non. Nee!'

Netter replied in a low mumble, which Belgi could not hear properly but recognised as her *I always get my own way* tone.

As Belgi turned from closing the door, Jessica took a step towards him and kissed him full on the lips. She placed one hand behind his head and an arm around his waist, kissing him harder until she felt his stubble rub against her chin. She squirmed her body against his; turning her back to Netter. Netter moved around and closer to the couple's faces. In her peripheral, Jessica saw Netter hold her hand to her mouth; she looked disappointed with the unfolding scene.

'Hey, guys. Come on. This is my idea. Come on guys. Like enough, please.'

Jessica allowed Belgi to return her kisses. She felt his tongue against her lips and began moaning in time with his breathing.

'No more guys. This isn't what I want.'

Jessica ignored Netter's hand on her shoulder. Netter moved between the couple. With her back against Jessica's side and levering her hands against Belgi - the couple embraced harder. Resisting Netter, Jessica theatrically moaned louder. Netter now moved her arm around Jessica's shoulder and pushed her free hand between their kissing mouths, making a physical barrier. As Jessica felt her friend's hand push against her own tongue, she released her embrace and pushed Belgi away, snorting into a laugh.

'And you said you were ready for this! You are so not ready Netter and you never will be, and you never should be. I told you so!'

Netter joined in nervously with the laughter and Belgi grinned at the women; he was not sure exactly what had just happened, but was happy to have been involved. Netter touched the slight rash on Jessica's chin with her fingertips.

'I was just worried in case he made your chin sore; that is all.' Jessica now guffawed into louder laughter, holding her friend in a reluctant embrace. Eventually, Netter dropped her head and admitted, 'Ok. Maybe the idea was better than the actual. But at least I get to spend the night in Posh Pod.' She smiled coyly to Jessica's laughter.

Following half an hour of the three lying silently in the dark, with only the stars and moon providing a little background glow through the roof window, Netter slid out of bed from next to

89

Belgi and gently climbed in with Jessica. Jessica faced away and on her side. Belgi pulled his thin duvet around his ears. Netter slowly inched backward until Jessica felt her own bottom nestle into the small of Netters back. Jessica stifled a giggle – it was like having a toddler sneak into mum's bed during the night. Composing herself and keeping completely still in the dark, Jessica pretended to sleep by regulating her breathing to an even and shallow rhythm. Netter continued to manoeuvre herself, until their backs were in contact, sharing a little body heat and comfort.

Jessica remembered how she would sleep with her sister in this position when visiting their grandparents as children. *Bookending.* Jessica closed her eyes and thought about her friends. Belgi she decided was a simple sole. An open and uncomplicated book. Netter was a lot more complex. She wanted to cook and be cooked for. Love and be loved. Be happy and spread happiness. It scared her to get too close to Belgi because she had so much more to offer the world. She pushed boundaries – continuously testing herself and testing others. Under attack, you would want Netter on your team. She was fearless and passionate. Jessica could not decide of whom Netter reminded her. Chris would know. Her eyes closed as she felt a safe sleep creep up and over her body.

Jessica untangled herself from Netter in the morning and left her friends sleeping. She packed her few belongings and made an early start to negotiate the almost continuous pothole, with only the odd stretches of tarmac, which was the road to Greece. She loved her small, low slung, baby blue two-seater sports car. The low suspension, urgent high-revving engine and skinny tyres of the Mazda did not like Albania.

Each evening Jessica wrote her journal and a list or itinerary for the following day, if travelling-on. The list included options for places to stay, eat, or visit; gleaned from the internet, guidebooks, or as she became more relaxed with strangers - from other travellers and locals. She often deviated or completely ignored the list, but it ensured she never found herself at a loss.

For her journal tonight, Jessica would have to decide if she liked Albania more than Slovenia.

Over the border in Greece, she headed for a nondescript and slightly rundown, large and almost empty council campsite. Nondescript except for the miles of pristine, wide sandy beach. Her allocated camping spot touched the sand and had a hard standing, water and domestic electrical socket. The shower blocks were mostly disgusting, with blocked toilets and leaking, broken showers, but Jessica soon developed a routine of spending the day on the beach and washing in the sea as the sun dipped; leaving the sea to rinse herself from a bottle of warm water previously collected from her dedicated standpipe. She stayed three nights. During the day she swam, sunbathed, and crashed the five-a-side football game played by the nine men and lads during lunch breaks on the beach outside a small boat repair yard. They were gentle with her for around five minutes of the first game until they learned, the hard way, she meant business. Even after shuffling the players around, Jessica's team always won.

The campsite pizza café was all too close to one of the toilet blocks for Jessica's liking, so she ate early at one of the daytime cafés within a short walk of her camp, or fried fresh fish on her tiny primus, from the wet-fish stall near the boatyard. Each afternoon she sat poised to write her moving-on list but struggled to decide where to go next. This was decision-time and would determine the remaining course of her adventure.

She had made a half-hearted date to meet with Albay in Athens – her Turkish friend from the Portsmouth ferryboat. He was handsome enough, but Jessica decided he was way too old and had probably forgotten all about her, anyway. Jessica realised she had to decide soon – she was running out of Europe.

She might make a large clockwise route to include the Greek Islands and Athens and then continue west to revisit a couple of her favourite spots before following the sun along the Spanish and Portuguese coasts. Or loop anticlockwise into Bulgaria and the mountains of Hungary, Austria and Germany. The hot beaches of Iberia, however, tugged at her heart.

Buying her filleted fish supper to fry on the sand near her tent in the dipping sun, Jessica decided – to *not* decide. She would press on until she was knocking on the door of the Middle East before making a snap decision to turn left or right, north or south. She stopped outside the boatyard and called over one of the footballers to say goodbye. Soon all the players had collected around her and each shook hands, wishing her a safe journey and telling her their names as if she might remember. Halfway back to the camp, the youngest lad of around seventeen-years-old ran up from behind her, panting. He held a posy of wildflowers, crimped together with a square of tinfoil, presumably salvaged from a lunchbox. He called her name and held out the flowers. Behind him at the gates of the yard stood the eight others in a line, watching. Blushing deeply, he bowed his head, brushed his heart and ran back to work.

After supper, Jessica packed away everything she did not need for the night and taking her When In Roam book and her journal, sat cross-legged on the bedroll spread on the warm sand. She had surrendered her previous book to the Albanian book swap shelf. In another life, she would have kept the present from her sister; Rapid Eye Movement by Amanda Sheridan had been a gripping read. Now, however, she had thrown herself into the minimum baggage life of a backpacker. With Jessica's healthy bank balance and a car, Pamdiana Jones may not agree with her backpacker self-definition, but she was in no hurry to survive on just white rice.

Jessica had carefully torn the first page from Rapid Eye Movement, containing her sister's note, and slipped it into her journal. She now unfolded the rescued bookmark she had used since Portsmouth and unfolded the old note – her 'The Start Of My New Life' list. It smelt of the perfume she shared with Amara, and Jessica blushed at the sudden memory of their hooking-up following an office Christmas party. She read the list again, adding a couple of ticks. She laughed at the inappropriate cartoon images Amara had drawn – mostly of male and female body parts. Then she wept, just a little; she was desperate to call Chris, although he had not made the effort. Tomorrow would be a fresh day and the turning point for the rest of her adventure. She held the posy of flowers to her nose, replacing the smells of home with the smells of her adventure.

2016 - The Start Of My New Life

1. Work ✓ - Finished at the Company. Take a long break and then find something I love to do; helping people or looking after animals. Rabbits or Blind Dogs.

2. Chris ✓ - Moved on from Chris. Take back control of my life. Make my own decisions. Don't lean on Amara, now that Chris has gone.

Lean on me as much as you want, my love!

3. Flat ✓ - Moved on. Buy or rent bigger, or maybe ask Landlord for my tiny flat back if new tenants cannot squeeze in.

4. Travel Europe ✓ A Road Trip. Thelma And Louise. (Or just Thelma). *And beyond Europe.*

5. Make awesome new friends ✓ *for life*

6. Wild Camp ✓ *And go wild*

7. Meet a rich, handsome, guy *your own age!* Maybe more mature *Fall in love* Or lust!

8. Stay in the poshest ever boutique hotel and pamper myself *and buy a holiday home – aim for the stars*

9. Swim in a waterfall *and be dried by the sun* or a hunk

10. Just Live A Little *and stay safe* Or at least stay alive

11. Prioritise myself *over and above anyone else – you are the most important*

12. Wear a soldier's uniform and fire his gun *kinky! fight him for it first*

13. Fall back into your friend's arms – I will always be ready to catch you

CHAPTER 8 – RICH AND HANDSOME

The following day started dull with occasional spits of rain. Jessica kept the soft-top of her sports car closed and the heating on – more for comfort than heat. She sang along to her Spotify playlist, but she would rather have been in her tiny flat, cooking for Chris. Jessica also remembered, with a smile, the slim and toned Jason Taylor from the Cinque Terre.

She concentrated on the road ahead; the passing scenery and glimpses of the Thracian Sea holding little interest - the water looked dull and uninviting, almost menacing. Jessica punched a motel address into her sat-nav at around two-thirds of the journey towards the Turkish border. She intentionally passed the turning to Athens and Albay, and she now wanted to touch the very edge of Europe. She had been premature in ticking the *Travel Europe* entry on her list and felt the adventure would come crashing down if she did not fulfil the prophecy by completing the trip. She contemplated selling her car in Alexandroupoli and flying home. Home to Guildford, perhaps.

Thankfully, the following morning proved bright and clear. Jessica could not face her breakfast, a bad diet sign, but felt much lighter in her mood.

The sea now sparkled in the early sun. With the roof down and the heater on full again, she powered along the road towards the bottom right-hand corner of Europe and the end of the first part of her adventure.

Not impressed with the outskirts of Alexandroupoli, Jessica eased her way through the traffic towards the historic port area and the famous lighthouse. After skirting the pedestrian area and not understanding the array of tow-truck signs, she eventually found a secure looking car park. She did her best to chat-up the attendant until he agreed she could tuck her compact car into a gap in the staff-only parking, close to the office and night attendant. She re-packed her day-bag to include a few overnight provisions, changed into her loose trousers with the more modest bikini-top under her open and knotted striped shirt, before making her way down a dingy alleyway towards the harbour area.

The world recession had hit Greece hard and away from tourist hotspots, the town looked sad and unloved. The alley became dingier as Jessica walked downhill, but she did not worry about becoming lost, with gravity pulling her toward the sea. Turning a sharp corner, Jessica hit a block-end. Turning around to retrace her steps, she started back up the hill towards a teenage girl dressed as a local might, but holding a tourist map. She spoke to Jessica whilst pointing at the map. As Jessica slowed to look at the map, while already holding up an apologetic hand to show the girl she was also lost, the girl grabbed and tugged at Jessica's bag. Jessica tugged back and as the couple spun around, she saw four young men stood across the alley blocking her exit. Three looked bored and one grinned.

The young girl now presented a distraction for Jessica at a time she needed to concentrate. Much harder than probably necessary, Jessica delivered a single jab to the girl's left temple, who fell backward into a row of bins. The four males did not look toward the crumpled heap on the floor. All four walked towards Jessica. Grinning male held a huge serrated hunting-knife and Jessica saw that another held a craft knife. Rather than turn her back and run further into the dead-end alley, Jessica faced her assailants. She brought her leather day-bag over her chest as a shield.

'Look, just take the money; please leave my journal.'

Jessica spoke as calmly as she could manage. None of the males appeared interested in the bag and Jessica realised this mugging had escalated into a potential personal assault, or far worse. She backed herself between the bins to offer some protection to her flanks and shrank down on to her bent left leg as if cowering, her bag now held in front of her face as she concentrated on Grinner's approaching feet. When her assailant was less than an arm's length away, Jessica launched herself forward off her left leg and, pushing the bag into his face, landed heavily onto the top of his left foot. Jessica felt and heard the bone and tendons crush and snap as he immediately buckled.

He fell forward onto his hands, Jessica stamped on to his right hand, breaking the fingers and trapping the knife he was holding. Steadying herself against the bin to her left, she repeatedly kicked him in the face. The first kick caught him squarely on the chin and probably knocked him out, her kicks now keeping his head off the ground like a football. The third or fourth kick shattered his teeth. His friends trampled the girl to reach Jessica, thankfully the male with the craft knife was shielded by the second male who Jessica protected herself from using the bag. The fourth male peeled off and clambered over the bins to her right, toward her most exposed side.

A shout pierced the cacophony of the fight as a well-dressed older man, obviously not associated with these males, stood further up the alley. The distraction lasted for a moment, but with all heads turned towards the man, Jessica ducked under the arm of one assailant, rammed the bag against the knife-carrying hand of the next and dropping the bag, ran up the alley.

She screamed, 'Run! Knife!' as she sped past the older man and glimpsing the sea to her left, ran between two buildings toward the main street and safety. Jessica saw a uniform ahead and screamed again, 'Police! Help!'

The traffic warden brought her radio to her face. At that same moment, Jessica realised her have-a-go-hero was not following and turned to retrace her steps. The traffic warden shouted for two men leant against a tow-truck to investigate, which they did clutching large spanners, as the traffic warden gripped Jessica's arm. As this second part of the incident unfolded, her hero walked from between the two buildings, holding Jessica's bag. The man Jessica now recognised as Albay Salepci.

'Miss! Your bag. You dropped it.'

'Albay! Are you ok? What happened? Why didn't you run? How did you retrieve my bag?' Jessica felt inside to make sure her journal was safe.

Albay smiled, and then his face broke into a wide grin. He leaned forward and scooped the evil-eye pendant from Jessica's chest, rubbing the heavy glass charm between his finger and thumb.

'Ha! My pretty Miss Jessica, I did not realise it is you. Fancy, fancy. I said Nazar would bring you safely to me.'

'A bit less dramatic would have been good, Albay.'

Albay shrugged and curled his lip in dismissal. 'You look unharmed; indeed you look lovely. Nazar has worked well, for us.'

He cupped Jessica's cheek and she twisted her face to kiss his palm – in a more intimate way than she had intended. The traffic warden released Jessica's arm as Albay pulled her into a gentle hug, wrapping his arms around her.

'You are safe now, *Kizim.*'

Jessica's heart pumped and her body trembled. As the adrenalin rush eased, she felt she might cry but was determined to look the strong woman that she was, in front of a gathering crowd.

'Missus and you sir must wait for police. Stay here.'

Albay nodded to the traffic warden and spoke in Greek, leading Jessica towards a stone bench as the warden set off toward a police car, which had just arrived. At the stone bench, Albay continued to lead Jessica across the harbour car park to rejoin the cobbled road that led through an arch and into the pedestrian area.

'Albay! We need to talk to the police. We need to wait.'

'Why *Kizim*? You have your bag, you are not harmed.'

'Albay! They attacked me, they could have killed us. There are two injured criminals and three others in that alley.'

'Exactly, Jessica. How is your Greek? That poor girl is in a bad way. I think the man is breathing, but you injured him.' He spoke with a grin as if this was a good thing. 'You have some serious explaining, young lady. I can take you back to the police if you like. Personally…' Albay bobbed his head from side to side as if weighing up the situation '… personally, I would keep walking.'

They walked together through the old harbour area, past trinket shops and cafes. Albay had one arm around Jessica's shoulders and the free hand leading her by the forearm. He gripped her lightly but led her firmly. Turning down a wider cobbled street towards the waterfront, Albay led her past an expensive clothes boutique and into the forecourt of a stone constructed hotel, a converted customhouse or warehouse. A young man immediately appeared next to Albay, showing him to the shaded table which Albay had clearly already selected for himself. To the right of them, as they faced back toward the gate, was rest of the beautifully laid-out forecourt with the entrance to reception. To their left, over a low wall, lapped the sea. They sat together, Albay holding the back of her chair, his other hand not leaving her forearm. Once sat, he swapped, holding her hand.

'My God, what have you done to your hand, Albay?'

'Oh, is nothing. Maybe I trip and fall, running away.'

A white linen napkin appeared from the attending waiter, but before Albay could wrap his hand, Jessica held it in hers, checking each finger and knuckle. Only half of the blood was Albay's. As Jessica gently dabbed at his hand with the moistened napkin, she studied a large round signet ring with a dagger design, now encrusted with blood. The receptionist appeared with a first aid box.

'Enough!'

Albay dragged his hand free. The two members of staff snapped to attention before backing away.

'Stay here!'

Jessica was surprised at the severity of this gentle man's voice. Albay collected the first aid box and disappeared into reception. After a few minutes, he returned to the table, his hand washed and taped with a square of gauze.

'Sorry, Miss Jessica. I dislike blood; I am not annoyed. Thank you for your concern, but you are the real veteran of today's battle.'

'So you fought the three men left standing and won? And you did that for me, to retrieve my bag?'

'Salep and Ginger, please.' The waiter disappeared. 'You will like this drink, it is for winter, but is good for a shock.'

'Albay!'

'Ok, Miss Jessica. They ran at me, to escape. Maybe I punched one in self-defence.'

Jessica was not convinced. She leant towards him, turning her head against his chest and draping her arms around his neck.

'My hero Albay. And please call my Jess, not Miss.'

'And you are my hero, Jess. Please, you must call me Al.'

The hotel was half-full of guests and staff. Albay sent the young waiter to retrieve Jessica's car and relocate it to the hotel car park immediately outside the pedestrian zone. The waiter also fetched Jessica's rucksack and, slightly awkwardly, the open carrier bag of Jessica's laundry.

'You must stay here, Jess. At least for tonight. I will make you feel safe, you have had a shock.'

'Sorry Al, but absolutely no way. I will find a small bed-and-breakfast; this beautiful hotel is a little over my budget.'

'I show you something.'

Albay took Jessica to his rooms, up a flight of stone steps and along a panelled corridor with a heavily beamed ceiling. Albay had a suite at the end with a sitting room overlooking the harbour town and a bedroom overlooking the sea. The bedroom had two huge four-poster beds, each aligned with a deep window looking out to sea. Between the windows stood a set of French doors, opening on to a balcony. The enormous bathroom included a double roll-top bath aligned with a glass door overlooking the same balcony and out to sea, double vanity units, his and hers toilets and even separate bidets and a double shower. The floor was the same soft pink stone as the bedroom. There was a leather sofa and a low bath stand in keeping, which acted as a drinks table.

'You must not be offended by what I am to say, Miss Khan. And you will only need to say no. Perhaps you could stay in the bedroom and I sleep in the sitting room. For one or two nights, before you continue your journey to Turkey.'

'Mr Salepci, I am not offended and yes please, I would like that, thank you.' However, Jessica was not looking to sleep in separate rooms.

Following an afternoon in the hotel pool and a backpacker's hour-long soak in the bath with glasses of Prosecco and all of the bath products provided, Jessica changed into her gingham dungarees. Although quite flattering and when she wanted a little revealing, she felt underdressed in this hotel. The guests, including her host, were most definitely the beautiful set. She tied her silk throw around her waist to give some flounce and met Albay in the forecourt.

'I am popping out to the shops, Al. I will see you later. You cannot come, as I might want to buy you a present.'

Albay smiled and, along with several of the other guests, watched Jessica leave the hotel. Even in Beautiful-Boutique-Hotel-World, Jessica turned heads.

Following a leisurely stroll around the harbour town, she found herself back in the clothes boutique next to the hotel. The assistant approached Jessica.

'Madam?'

'I am looking for a present, for a special friend and on a special occasion.'

'Of course, madam. So you must tell me please, what is her size and what is the occasion?'

'It is for a man. And I am the occasion.'

Jessica bought several silk items by the same designer, almost doubling her travel wardrobe –

the complete purchase filled only the smallest of shop-boxes. Jessica wondered if the cocktail dress, pyjama set and two pairs of underwear could almost roll up tightly enough to fit into the matching silk clutch. Sometimes, she decided, less is more.

Jessica strolled down the stone stairs into reception, carefully watching her step and wearing the new Cinderella-style evening shoes with a higher heel than she might normally wear. The shoe had a delicate and intricate design of glass beads and crystals over a lacquered blue cutout fabric revealing much of her foot and which picked out the background colour of her dress. The crystals caught the light and matched more of the deeper blues and dark reds of the dress. The dress hugged her body perfectly, with pencil straps that stayed in place without slipping and a hem that fell to just above her knee. The dress split the entire length of her left thigh, the split then closed by a delicate lace panel, which also trimmed the hem, the low bust line and the high waist. The silk pattern was moody blue, resembling a tropical sky after a storm, and covered with navy-blue leopard print - each print edged with a fiery red, giving an overall jungle-evening impression. From a distance or in the bedroom, the delicate silk dress could have been mistaken for a sexy nightdress and this was not by accident.

Pound-for-pound, sidling up to Albay from the reception would not have made effective use of the ridiculous price tag. Therefore, Jessica took a moment to stroll through the forecourt to the hotel gate on the pretence of admiring the honeysuckle, now throwing-out scent into the slight, cool, evening breeze. After exchanging a few words with the waiter positioned at the gate, Jessica turned and slowly scanned the tables to find Albay, purposely starting from the opposite side to where she knew he would be sitting. As her eyes eventually fell on Albay, he had already stood and held out both hands to show his admiration. She returned his enormous smile and sparkling eyes, before walking back across the forecourt and into an embrace.

'*Kizim, askim.* Jessica, you are so beautiful. I am honoured to invite you to my table.'

'You like your present then?'

Jessica saw his poker face slip for the first time, as a hint of blush coloured his cheeks.

'All *Bayram* in one moment.' He dipped his head in a bow. 'Sorry, but I must stare at you all night, *seftalim.*'

'All *night,* Al?'

Albay stood for a moment seeming unable to understand, before shaking his head with the tinkling giggle of a much younger man; stepping aside, he pulled back Jessica's chair. As soon as they sat, a waiter appeared and took the drink order - Jessica allowing Albay to choose a small bottle of Raki to share. The drink appeared with water, ice and a plate of chilli meze, a yoghurt meze and olives. Jessica picked at the meze as the waiter elaborately prepared their drinks, adding water until the clear liquor turned milky and placing the ice carefully into each glass with a flourish. Stepping back, the waiter moved to place the bottle and ice onto a serving table, Albay signalled for him to leave it on their table and so clarifying that they were not to be disturbed.

'My friend. This is our national drink,' holding his glass to the candle to show the milky white liquid. 'we call it lion's milk. *Serefe!*'

'Then *serefe*, to you, my lion.'

'My goodness, no. It is a Turkish custom that the oldest male at the table starts the conversation when raki is poured. So I will say: you are the lioness. For a moment today, I felt a little sorry for those unfortunate hyenas.' Albay gently teased with a light, joking voice.

'Notwithstanding them being a gang of five with weapons attacking me down a dark alley, the thing I found most distressing was the blank looks. Drugged-up do you think?'

'Almost certainly. This is a lost generation, since the economic collapse. Maybe we are better off in Turkey *insallah,* but *Yunanistan* has it very bad.'

'*Yunanistan*?'

'Sorry, how we say Greece.'

Jessica took this opportunity to glimpse behind the armour. Albay was deft at avoiding any kind of scrutiny, meaning that they had spoken mostly about neutral topics or about Jessica – a subject that she was also most interested.

'So you are Turkish? Why are you in Greece? What do you do? Are you married, family? What are the chances of you walking down an alley just when I needed you most Al, just what are the chances?'

Albay sat back in his chair and gave a genuine laugh.

'I am not so interesting, *tatlim*. Some of my family live in Turkey, I am Turkish, but some of my family live here. We are in Eastern Thrace, just now Greece occupies it, but before it is Turkish.'

'Occupied? A strong word.' Albay shrugged.

'We think it is rude to talk politics with a lady.'

'We think it is rude to patronise guests. In England, women have the vote and everything!'

'Of course. I am so rude, I live in a different generation. Oh, and women had the vote in Turkey, before England.' Albay smiled and Jessica managed a sexy mock-scowl.

'And?'

'And I am mostly retired from the family business.'

'I assumed military.'

'*Evet kizim* and also the military, we all serve.'

'And?'

Albay laughed a soft chuckle. 'I have a large extended family and one son. I still have an elderly mother, she lives in Turkey.'

'And?'

'Is everything, my beautiful. Please, we must talk about your travels to Turkey.'

'And, Albay? And?'

'I am not married.'

Good!

'Ok, for now. What shall we eat, is the kitchen Turkish? Can you choose for me? No octopus, you should try the prawns and crab in Albania, my travels have been so good Al and I started to feel down, but now I am sat here with you and I am not planning on going to Turkey, I doubt it will be my bag, I am glad you like your present.' Jessica had seen Albay drop his gaze and scan her bare shoulders and the low neckline of her dress.

Albay's eyebrows rose in surprise at the speed that the conversation zigzagged and of Jessica's talking.

Albay ordered more mezes, small plates of food to share. '*Ahtapot yok!*' to the waiter. 'So, why not octopus, it tastes so good if cooked by a Turk!'

'I know Al, but they are so clever, so empathetic. They are affectionate to other animals and the fisherman and they try to make friends with the chef, before being brutally murdered, by their new friends.'

Albay looked genuinely shocked. 'I shall never eat octopus again, in honour of my lioness.'

The couple smiled at each other and Jessica, only just realising they were holding hands, squeezed his gently.

The mezes continued to appear - rich oily aubergine, bean salad, fresh chilli paste, baked mushroom, crab, small fish. Jessica spoke mostly as she ate, occasionally forking food directly into Albay's mouth and even using her fingers to feed him olives, which he had not requested. Her feeding other people who had not asked infuriated Chris, but Jessica did it without realising and Albay either did not mind or was too polite to object.

Occasionally Jessica fell silent and before she could ask Albay for more information about himself, he would talk more about Turkey. More meze arrived – stuffed mussels, stuffed vine leaves, stuffed peppers, refreshing cucumber in yogurt and palate-cleansing melon. Cold liver and seemingly raw meatballs appeared next; Jessica tried a little but decided she had had enough. Immediately stopping eating himself, Albay gestured for the table to be cleared and ordered

Turkish coffee with sweet pastry baklava, dripping with honey.

'You must go to Turkey *tatlim*. The Black Sea coast is so sophisticated; you will fit in well. We have mountains, waterfalls. We have cities of cave dwellers. We have Roman, Greek and Byzantium ruins. You are too late to ski. The Aegean coast is so Turquoise it will break your heart; you cannot go to Turkey without falling in love. The people are beautiful and friendly, you are never alone in Turkey. And the food, the food, the food!'

Jessica giggled and hiccupped to the taste of aniseed raki. 'But is it safe, especially for a girl on her own? And isn't it all a bit, you know, Muslim? And there is a war going on and army on the streets. And can you get a drink and am I not a little... immodest, would I have to wear a scarf?'

'Only people who have not visited Turkey, dislike Turkey. We are strictly secular – we do not permit even a librarian or a schoolteacher to wear the hijab. The army police the countryside and are less corrupt than the civilian police – even than your own police; you will see no street crime! No, we drink like fish but do not become drunk in public. Immodest? Are you not a little immodest at home?' Jessica widened her eyes with indignation but reluctantly accepted the accusation. 'The war is as far from Istanbul as Istanbul is from Vienna. We are a massive sub-continent-of-a-country – we have more flora and fauna in Turkey than the whole of Europe added together, different species and actual volume! If it is good enough for Father Christmas, well - Jessica Khan will be just fine.'

Jessica took a gulp of Turkish coffee before spitting it back into her cup, wiping her tongue on a napkin and gulping water to wash away the muddy sediment.

'I apologise my sweet, I should have said – it must settle.'

The waiter took the cup away, Albay replaced it with his own and a replacement for his arrived, once brewed.

'So, Father Christmas has visited Turkey? I hope they didn't kebab Rudolph!'

'Father Christmas is Turkish. St Nicholas has his house close to my mother's side of the family. And your mayor of London, soon to be Prime Minister, is also Turkish.'

Jessica giggled from behind her hand, still removing coffee fines from her tongue. 'So now, I know you are fibbing, barmy Boris Johnson will never be Prime Minister. Next, you will tell me the Queen of England and St. George are Turkish!'

Albay joined in with Jessica's laugh. 'No *askim,* you have me there. Your Queen is German, but yes, St. George is Turkish.'

They had started to eat early; the dishes kept arriving and conversation flowed like the wine, mostly about Jessica, her travels and Turkey. After a walk around the old part of the harbour, they headed for the bedroom at gone midnight, together. Albay busied himself in the sitting room while Jessica used the bathroom. She changed into her new silk peach pyjama top and selected one of the two pairs of matching shorts. She pulled on the longer shorts, which stopped mid thigh, and twirled in front of the mirror. They suited her build and accentuated her slim calves and ankles.

Jessica rolled her eyes at herself *who am I kidding?* and swapped the shorts for an extremely brief pair of matching silk and lace bottoms. She did not call to Albay, but leant against the open French door, watching the waves gently lap and the small local fishing boats head out to work. Jessica had already broached sleeping arrangements and Albay graciously accepted her

118

insisting that neither should sleep on the sofa and if he were to insist, then it must be Jessica. Albay knocked lightly on the door and when Jessica did not answer, cautiously entered the bedroom. Seeing Jessica framed in the doorway, he cleared his throat and made for the bathroom to shower, returning in pyjama shorts and a bathrobe left to gape open; his cotton shorts patterned with prints of astronauts, Jessica barely stifled a giggle.

Jessica gestured to the twin four-poster doubles and insisted Albay choose first. Leaving the French Windows open to the night air, she then slipped into bed. Under slightly different circumstances, she would have fallen almost instantly to sleep as her head sunk into the soft pillow, but not tonight. With the couple on their backs and looking up at the same beamed ceiling in almost darkness, Jessica spoke first.

'So Albay, I do not believe in coincidences. Why were you in the alley at the exact moment I needed you most?'

'It is a coincidence, *tatlim.* You would not remember me *not* being there. You only remember because I *was* there and so you will remember this coincidence for a long time, or perhaps your entire life. Let me give you another example. I chose my bed closest to the door because I am a gentleman and because I usually sleep in this bed. By coincidence, you chose the same bed to sleep in tonight and I promise, you will not forget this night for a very long time, either.'

Jessica slept late and eventually waking, found Albay on the balcony working on his laptop in front of a huge breakfast of more small dishes.

'Please.' Albay stood to pull back Jessica's chair. 'I have started a little, sorry.'

'Blimey Al! What on earth is all of this?'

Jessica was conscious that neither had leant to kiss the other and now that immediate moment of spontaneity was lost; it would feel too awkward to try now. In the same way that she might feel hungry in the morning following a big supper, so she felt like leading Albay back to bed following their previous night of lovemaking, but that would not now happen.

'This is a traditional Village Breakfast. It can change around Turkey, but today we have flatbread, sausage, cheese rolls, jam, honey, white cheese, yellow cheese, cheese like your cottage cheese from goats but is dry, boiled egg, sorry I

120

ate the fried egg,' Albay smiled apologetically 'but they will make you more. You can see green olives, black olives, almonds, simit bread rings with sesame seeds, you see tomatoes and cucumber, some hazelnut spread, some nuts roasted in honey, some chillies and a little chilli paste with tomato, we call ezme.'

The teapot comprised a copper kettle sat over a tea light with a second kettle of water, which fitted over the teapot. The tea glasses were tulip-shaped and served with tiny sugar spoons, sat in a fretwork copper saucer to match the kettles.

'My mother will make you Kuyma for breakfast, but not at this hotel.' Albay noticed the sudden look of surprise on Jessica's face. Not realising it was at the mention of meeting his mother, he continued. 'It is like your porridge, perhaps a little. But with cheese and butter and cream. And not oats, but cornmeal. And the cheese is old.'

'So, nothing like porridge then?' Jessica smiled but, following the reference to meeting his mother, she struggled to meet his eye. 'I have decided to visit Turkey Al. Perhaps you will help me write a list.' Jessica suddenly felt childish and, sat in just pyjamas in front of this fully clothed and older man, she felt herself blush. 'You know, like a route.'

'Yes, of course. I will have reception find us a tourist map later. You must ask me anything. I am visiting soon, perhaps one or two weeks. Perhaps Nazar will bring you to me again.'

'There is something I want to ask you, Al. You will not want to answer and I cannot make you.' Studying the piece of bagel simit she dipped into hazelnut paste, Jessica continued, 'You were shot.'

Albay laughed and gently squeezed her wrist. 'Yes, my sweet. Three times on two occasions.'

'Does it hurt?'

'Only when a pretty girl looks at the scars.'

Jessica had seen a groove or gouge on his left waist, an area of rounded scar tissue on his left hip, and another round entry wound to his right shoulder – piercing and distorting a tattoo of a dagger or a short bayonet, the blade barbed like a lightning strike. There was an exit wound on his right side, presumably from the shoulder wound, and a large area of skin grafts above his left buttock. She mustered enough courage to hold his gaze.

'Is ok now. I have a nice new hip and nothing else is a problem.'

'And?'

Albay looked a little confused.

'I am not married.' Jessica did not laugh at the joke. 'I was a soldier, we all have to serve. I was shot twice in Kosovo and once in the east, near the Iranian border. They thought I had bad luck, so pensioned me. I had to agree, things were not going well!' He laughed again, alone.

'Kosovo?'

'Turkey is a NATO country. In fact, the largest NATO army outside of the USA.'

Jessica was not convinced of either claim, but neither was she in the mood to interrogate him on world politics, just at this moment.

'How will you travel to Turkey Albay, to see your mother?'

'I will fly. Maybe next week.'

'Mr Selapci, you only have to say no and I will understand.' Jessica imitated the tone he had used to discuss sharing the room, which had then led to so much more. 'Rather than spend an hour sipping wine in, no doubt, first-class air travel - do you fancy spending a couple of weeks cramped into my tiny car with no air-con, eating dust and driving through Turkey with me?'

'Miss Khan, it will honour me. Thank you, *disi aslanim.*'

Jessica wanted to add that a few more nights in the best hotels, some intimacy, lovely company and an expert guide – did not constitute agreeing to meet his mother; she decided to keep that conversation for later on the road trip.

CHAPTER 9 – BEYOND EUROPE

Jessica spent an hour carefully packing her bag and writing her journal. The hotel took it upon itself to raid her wardrobe and drawer when she was visiting the lighthouse, leaving Albay alone to work. Her well-worn clothes were now in better shape than since leaving Portsmouth, with food oil and sun oil stains removed, loose buttons refastened and hems re-sown. Everything was pressed and folded or rolled for packing. On her way back to the hotel she visited the car to check oil, water and tyres, sorting the boot and packing some items under the seats to make room for her guest's bag.

Following a light supper of shared Greek Salad in a local café, they retired to the hotel early. Jessica felt unusually self-conscious and selected the longer pyjama shorts; slipping into their bed before Albay was ready. She closed her eyes for a moment to the gentle sound of Albay packing his bag for the morning and drifted to sleep. During the early hours, she awoke to find Albay in the second bed.

She woke again early morning and Albay later found her sat impatiently on the balcony. She called down to reception for two takeaway breakfasts. Albay laughed at her enthusiasm to visit the country she had considered 'not her bag' but dressed and made ready as quickly as possible.

'What about all this?' Jessica gestured to clothes in the wardrobe and various belongings, including a small printer, on the desk and dressing table.

'Is ok. Hotel will look after, until my next visit.'

Jessica blinked widely.

'Blimey! Not in the Travelodges I stay in.'

Seeing Jessica fidgeting in her chair, Albay took one sip of hot instant coffee and gestured with arms held wide. '*Hazir.*'

Jessica sprang from her seat, kissed him on the lips and grabbing her bag, made for the door; Albay close behind.

With the car boot open, Albay gently eased a wooden box covered in bubble-wrap to the rear of the compartment, carefully stacking Jessica's beach bag, towels and other soft objects around it to cushion any knocks. He then added his leather barrel bag.

'You travel with a wooden chest. Not a pirate, are you?'

'I have been accused of worse, but no. My father bought my mother this old "portable" radiogram on honeymoon. It has been in my spare room, broken, for years. I restored the box. My friend could not fix the old valve radio, but he has added a tuner to fit the old knobs and using the same speaker. Mother will never know.'

'You are a lovely son, Al.' Jessica squeezed his waist in a hug and kissed the tip of his nose. She held open the passenger door for Albay, ran to the driver's side, and soon they headed for the border and out of Europe.

Reaching a long queue of lorries for the border, Jessica drove slowly down the outside lane and joined the much shorter line of cars. Albay plugged his phone charger pad into the car's USB port and removed the evil-eye charm from the mirror, laying it across his phone. Jessica smiled at him fussing with the charm; it was hardly distracting.

As they waited, Albay explained to Jessica which car documents she would need, where to buy car insurance (he would pay) and how to buy the entry visa for ten pounds - she had a ten-pound note tucked into her coin tray for emergencies. She did not see Albay's call notification, but he swiped his phone and immediately began an urgent conversation in Greek. They crept forward two spaces in line before Albay jumped from the car and took his bag from the boot; continuing to talk animatedly into the phone. A car horn beeped from behind, Albay closed his door as Jessica moved forward another space. They were now one space back from the front, as a border guard approached. Albay nodded at the guard before going to Jessica, kissing the top of her head.

'Sorry, my love. A problem, I must leave you now. I will call you.'

Before Jessica could speak, Albay crossed towards a taxi dropping passengers at the border; the guard called Jessica forward, the car behind beeped again.

'Miss, all ok?' Jessica nodded, still speechless. 'My father is same. Probably left the gas on, or forgot his slippers.'

'Yeah, fucking prick.' Jessica mumbled in reply.

The women exchanged knowing smiles as they beckoned Jessica forward to the booth, holding her passport. Border control waved her through to Turkey.

Turkish border control directed Jessica into a parking space and led her to a tiny interview room. Behind the desk sat two guards; on Jessica's side of the table sat a man, reading a Turkish newspaper. Nobody introduced themselves.

'Passport!'

The guard flicked through every page, holding some to the light at an angle. His colleague stared at Jessica.

'English?'

Jessica gestured to the passport he was holding.

'I am a U.K. citizen, yes.'

His female colleague spoke. 'Not English?'

Jessica sighed. 'Yes, English. Is everything ok?'

'Why do you go to Turkey, where are you staying, when do you go home?'

Jessica spread the hotel tourist map onto the desk and pointed at the places she hoped to visit. Neither guard looked at the map.

'Who do you know in Turkey? Why are you not with your husband?'

'I am not a hundred percent certain that is any of your business. But as you ask, I do not know anyone in Turkey and I am not married. Apparently, I'm too flighty to marry but absolutely fine to *bed*. You know the type, love-me and leave-me.'

Both guards listened impassively to Jessica's speech.

'You will not go to the east, understand?'

Jessica nodded. The guard added a stamp to the passport and wrote a number, taken from his laptop, into a blank section left by the ink crest.

As Jessica stood, the colleague spoke again. 'You are not our profile for concern, Jessica Miss, but girls from England come to Turkey to marry Islamic State fighters. You are quite dark-skinned; you will be stopped at every roadblock. Leave extra time for your journey.'

Jessica very nearly returned to Greece, but the queue of cars was much longer than on the Greek side. Sighing to herself, she pulled on to the wide and almost empty road, driving past a small village before joining the major trunk road east and south, avoiding Istanbul and heading towards the Gallipoli Peninsular. By the time she reached the highway interchange, she had braked hard to avoid a tractor, slowed for a herd of sheep, run over a kitten chasing its mother across the road, sounded her horn for a farmer to pull his donkey to the side and side-swiped a dog. The dog did not seem to mind – sleeping on the main road where he did, Jessica assumed he was used to being driven into.

Jessica found the Gallipoli peninsular mostly open farmland and scrubland, and although beautiful, Jessica imagined it would be a bleak, empty place in winter. She followed a camping sign to a café, with space for a few tents around the back. As she pulled in, she spotted the now-familiar yellow camper belonging to Belgi and Netter.

In his best Dick Van Dyke cockney accent, Belgi called across to Jessica.

'If it ain't the bad penny! Well Gawd bless me soul!'

The couple had returned from a private battlefield tour with a guide they had tracked down through an old on-line Daily Telegraph newspaper article. He previously guided world dignitaries around the First World War landings and battlefields and lectured in New Zealand and the U.K.. He discussed world politics with Prince Charles and joked with New Zealand's premier, John Key.

The three intercepted Kenan Bay as he left the café. They spoke for a short while and agreed to meet for breakfast the following morning. Jessica would then drive and Kenan would guide her around the battlefields with an emphasis on the ordinary soldier's tribulations, rather than the bigger political picture. Jessica's father had mentioned the landings several times over the years, usually when ranting about politicians trying to interfere with the military and preventing them from doing an honest day's work of killing foreigners.

With the car roof down and the relative silence punctuated only by calls to prayer, Kenan gave a gentle commentary, explaining why and how events unfolded during the doomed allied campaign and how this caused misery to the soldiers involved. The Turkish and allied soldiers grew a deep respect for each other and amongst the countless stories of heroics and barbarism, were heart-tugging examples of gentle kindness and compassion. Australia and New Zealand sent their shop assistant and farmer sons far away to die on these tiny battlefields – some as small as a couple of tennis courts, or narrow slither of beaches, and now the ANZACs claimed this campaign for their own. Statistically, the Turks suffered the greatest loss of life followed by the

British. Indian regiments and French also perished, but the wound sunk deep into the psyche and national conscience of Australasia and Kenan explained how they still pilgrimage to the area, especially at the end of April for Anzac Day.

Standing looking out across the Dardanelles, above Anzac Cove, Kenan pointed to a grassy knoll.

'I do this with my students. Go to the top of the small hill. You will see original trenches. Sit for a minute and read out the names on this sheet. Tell me at which point the names disappear.'

'Disappear?'

Jessica felt self-conscious but as they were alone she agreed. Perched on the rear revetment of a collapsing trench with her toes playing in the soft sandy silt, Jessica opened the sheet of paper. The page was dated and titled 'Men That Fell This Day In 1915'. Jessica scanned the lists of names by nationality, Australia being first alphabetically. There were no references, notes, explanations, or caveats. There were no ages or ranks, just lists of men's names, hundreds of names.

Feeling silly and stifling a giggle behind her hand, Jessica cleared her throat and began to read the names aloud. After twenty names her voice weakened; she continued to read name after name of dead men: sons, brothers, perhaps a few husbands and fathers. Jessica wiped her eyes with the back of her hand, but they welled again immediately. At less than one hundred names through the list, Jessica gave up and stared out to sea, waiting for her tears to dry in the salt breeze. Her toes rubbed something hard, and she retrieved a small metal cross measuring around one and a half inches.

Jessica handed Kenan the list, and he did not ask how far she had managed. She showed him the cross. Clearing her throat and trying not to sound so emotional, Jessica spoke.

'I found this. Is it a key, do you think?'

Kenan led the way to a large bronze plaque against a stone memorial.

'You were right to ask about the personal tragedy of war, my dear. It was to be the war to end all wars. The Turks in the trenches rained bullets onto the heads of these foreign invaders, and the young farmers from the other side of the world fired back. The air was thick with lead, like a cloud of locust. You have found where a Turkish bullet hit an allied bullet and fell to the ground, spliced together. You must keep this forever. You must tell your children about this madness.'

'Do the locals still hate the British for invading you like this?'

Kenan smiled.

'We are a strange people. We hold a grudge for generations about a fence, or a daughter falling in love with the wrong boy, but we seem to be more relaxed about wars.' He chuckled at the absurdity of his comment. 'Your young men did not want to come here to kill a Mehmet and our Mehmet did not want to kill your Johnny. If they had met in a bar, they would have bought each other a drink, not try to kill each other. Let me read this quote from our Kemal Ataturk, an Ottoman general and the father of the modern Turkish Republic.'

Kenan ran his finger over the bronze inscription before translating a brief passage.

'This is from a letter he wrote to the mother's of the fallen allies

'*Those heroes that shed their blood and lost their lives ... You are now lying in the soil of a friendly country. Therefore rest in peace. There is no difference between the Johnnies and the Mehmeti to us where they lie side by side in this country of ours. You, the mothers, who sent their sons from faraway countries, wipe away your tears. Your sons are now lying in our bosom and are in peace.*

After having lost their lives on this land, they have become our sons as well.'

The drive back to the café was muted. Jessica caught a glimpse of the proud young nation that Albay had referred to and despite every pedestrian, driver and animal on the road trying to kill her, she was going to like Turkey.

Kenan picked up the evil-eye charm resting on the phone charger pad, but dropped it immediately to the floor, cautiously touching the charger with his left hand.

'The charm is red hot, sorry to drop it. The charger feels cool, but perhaps a problem.'

Jessica unplugged the USB.

Back at camp, Jessica purchased three bottles of Efes Beer from the cafe and sat with Netter and Belgi by the camper. They small-talked about Turkey and their future travel plans, and Netter probed around the liaison with Albay. Jessica picked-up on a slight preoccupation in their mood but the couple appeared affectionate. Belgi left for more beers.

'All ok? Belgi ok?'

'Yeah, all good. He is nervous about driving tomorrow. I will drive to the train station, but he worries about driving back through Istanbul; the country roads are scary enough! Jessica, may I ask a big favour please?'

'No Netter, I will not join you and Belgi in the sack!' Both women laughed, and Netter brought her hands to cover her face in embarrassment. 'Even if it would be quite good fun.'

Jessica tried to prise Netter's hands away to enjoy her embarrassment but Netter kept them clamped to her face, giggling.

'Stop teasing me, Jess. Or at least wait until I have had more beer!' Jessica relented and sat back smirking. 'I want to ask. If you are still with Belgi when I call from my trip alone to Iran to, you know, finish everything, may I call you instead please, so you can tell him?'

'No, you bloody well cannot! You must call him yourself and no texting. Netter, what are you like?'

Netter nodded reluctantly. 'Who am I like, do you mean?'

'Are you sharing your find-a-phone location with Belgi? Here, you must with me.'

Jessica took Netter's phone and set the app on both so that Jessica could track her location throughout the trip to Iran.

'So girls. You are talking about me? Does it mean Jessica kisses me again, *s'embrasser*?'

Netter answered by swiping his head.

'I have a plan for tomorrow.' Jessica changed subjects. 'We take both vehicles to near Istanbul and park-up. I then drive you both to the train station to start Netter's Persian Odyssey. Belgi and I find somewhere central to crash and enjoy Istanbul for the night and I drive Belgi back to the camper on the following day.'

Belgi's eyes lit up at the possibility of avoiding driving through Istanbul and Netter nodded her approval, pleased that Belgi would not be alone should she decide to make the call.

'Also Jessica, I will drive to Cappadocia and live in a cave until Netter is ready for collection. You can visit me there.'

Albay had spoken about the UNESCO World Heritage Site, and Jessica immediately agreed.

Leaving the camper parked on the very edge of Istanbul, Netter sat on Belgi's lap for the drive into the megacity. They had moved all spare luggage from the Mazda into the camper, including Albay's heavy old radiogram which Jessica had forgotten she still held custody of, to make room for the three rucksacks. Belgi and Netter shrieked as Jessica wound the sports car between trucks, pedestrians, and horse and carts. The more they squealed, the louder Jessica laughed and faster she drove. They drove through two police roadblocks before hitting the city centre – both times the police stared at the three, before waving them on.

In mock desperation to alight the car, Netter and Belgi rolled out and on to the car park tarmac; Jessica just shrugged at their fear of the roads.

'C'mon guys! That was fun, what's up with you?'

Jessica stayed with the car to allow the couple a moment alone. Before going, the women hugged and Jessica hung the Turkish evil-eye charm around Netter's neck.

'To bring you back safely to me. Or if not to me, perhaps to Albay.'

'But I might not…' Netter glanced at Belgi before changing the ending to her sentence '… need it.'

'Netter, you are the bravest coward I have ever met. You must look after my charm for as long as it takes for us to meet again.'

Jessica and Belgi found a small hotel close to the Blue Mosque and spent rest of the day visiting the tourist sites. They employed an unofficial guide to show them around the Blue Mosque and then kept her for the day as she guided them around the Hippodrome, the Islamic Arts Museum and Sultanahmet Square. Belgi was no shopper, but Jessica thought he enjoyed the hustle and bustle of Arasta Bazaar and the labyrinth of tiny shops and boutiques around the mosque's cloisters. Leading them through the most unassuming of doors off the street, the three descended into the Basilica Cistern – a cathedral-like structure including towering buttresses, housing the city's reservoir; complete with anaemic coy carp and enough drips and ghostly echoes to give them nightmares for a week. They moved on to Hagia Sophia and their young guide brought the history to life, explaining how this was originally a church and Christian cathedral built in the early sixth century, before being converted to a mosque. It was now a museum, in this most secular of countries – with a ninety-seven percent Muslim population.

'Is like my country. Is beautiful, but is risk of crumbling. Perhaps the next earthquake will push it down. Or perhaps this president will make it a mosque again to please his uneducated Islamic friends from the countryside.'

The three hopped on to a tram, a clean air-conditioned oasis from the noise and bustle of Istanbul, before transferring to an old heritage tram and a short journey to Taksim Square. The guide pointed to a collection of higgledy-piggledy houses built on the centre island of a gyratory system.

'We have strange laws in Turkey and we hardly ever repeal old laws, it takes too long. The council makes it more difficult now, but it is still legal to build a house on any spare piece of the city or unused land during the hours of darkness. These people are Turkish Kurds from the east. They must not connect utilities, but perhaps they borrow some electricity from the pylons and some local properties let them run a hosepipe for water. They are always improving their community and some houses are quite comfortable. If they move out, then another Kurd, or nowadays perhaps a Syrian refugee, will move in at the same time. If the house is empty, the council will pull it down.'

'And the neighbours do not mind?'

The guide shrugged 'Why would they mind Jessica *hanim*? We all have to live somewhere. I looked at your BBC online; your government is worried about being overrun by the hundreds of refugees from Syria this year. Turkey has four million refugees from the conflict, all of them are allowed to travel throughout the country and look for work; they work hard. They are entitled to minimum wage. Or they can stay in the camps and try to go home as soon as is safe.'

Belgi spoke 'And they are Kurds, I thought the Turks dislike Kurds? Does the Turkish Army not fight the Kurds?'

'Turks dislike terrorists, Kurds dislike terrorists. Kurds are not terrorists, they just want freedom. Twenty percent of Turkish citizens are Kurdish and more voted for our current president than voted for all the Kurdish parties added together. Many of the Turkish soldiers killed in the east are Kurds, nearly half. I am Kurdish. It is like your Irish problem, Jessica. You were not fighting Ireland; you were not fighting the Irish, you were fighting the IRA.'

In a thick Yorkshire accent, Belgi added, 'No Blacks, No Irish, No dogs.'

The guide looked at Jessica with a quizzical frown.

142

'It is a note that landladies would put on their windows; not so long ago and not part of our history I am proud of. I guessed you treated your immigrants the same – scratch the liberal to smell the bigot underneath.'

'I am sure your friends in England and France are good, and I am not saying Turkish people are any better. We are short-tempered and hold grudges, but perhaps we have instructions from the Koran to extend the hand of welcome, for three nights at least.'

They ordered *Islak* with metal goblets of *Ayran* and sat a little way from the stall on the grass of Gezi Park. The sweet and spicy tomato sauce from the hamburgers dripped down their chins and the salty yoghurt *Ayran* rehydrated them, following a busy day in the heat. Following a walk around the square, with a commentary from Guide, Belgi asked to finish the trip in a hookah café. Both women agreed he could add a few crumbs from a cube he had bought outside the train station.

Passing around the hubble-bubble, Belgi inhaled twice the amount as the women; Jessica felt a rush from the marijuana and the strawberry flavoured tobacco-mix and did not want to feel ill, but was quite happy and relaxed with the small amount she took.

'So this is where you had the protests last year?'

'*Evet* Belgi. But, it was three years ago; times fly. First was protest about development and then was protest about how protestors were treated. It spiralled into protest against the government, corruption, the president, erosion of the secular state. Our president must tread carefully – you lose Istanbul, you lose Turkey.'

'How will it pan out, do you think? I mean, your president is a little, reactionary.' Jessica asked. Guide shrugged.

'One of three ways. The opposition party could win the next elections. This is unlikely, is like your Labour Party. David Cameron does terrible things with a pig's ear – it is not his fault that Labour is unelectable; it is Jeremy Corbyn's fault.
'Or the president could become much stronger and Turkey will become less secular, more Islamic. He now controls the media and police and is taking back the academic institutions from his old friend and now adversary, Fethullah Gulen. To me, the president and Gulen are the same anti-secular person, but they fell-out big time. They both think their own dick is bigger, perhaps.' Guide glanced at Belgi and blushed at her own language, the pot loosening her tongue.

'And the third way?' Jessica prompted. Guide leaned in closer,

'The Army.' Jessica and Belgi both went to speak, but Guide held a finger to her lips. She whispered. '*I* am like *Turkey*. The *Army* is like my big *brother*.' She took another drag on the water-pipe, looked around and leaned back in her chair.

'I am twenty-six, Jessica. I am a big girl now. I can look after myself and I do not need my brother to interfere with the way I run my life. But, I love him very much and I do trust him.

'Before I chose the wrong boyfriend, more than once. He supported me to change my mind, but I did not. So he changed my boyfriends' minds instead. He intervened. Perhaps he was right, but I am still annoyed, I need to make my own mistakes.

'Now I have a new boyfriend. He does not hold the same values as my brother. I am worried my brother will intervene again. I love my brother, but if I can, if I am strong enough, perhaps I will stand up to him, this time.'

The couple left Guide in Taksim Square, walking back towards their hotel.

'Twenty-six! I thought she was twelve when she first approached us by the Blue Mosque. At least I didn't offer her a bag of sweets.'

'Jess, do you think Netter will come back to me?'

Jessica slipped her arm through his.

'She will be fine Belgi, she can look after herself.'

'You know that is not what I mean. So you think she won't?'

'I didn't say that Belgi.'

'It doesn't matter. It was my best holiday romance ever. But, I will miss her. If she told you, that she would not come back to me, would you also tell me, Jessica?'

'No, my darling, I would not.'

Belgi sighed and shrugged.

'And I got to *snog-ged* the prettiest girl I ever met.'

Jessica turned to Belgi and draped her arms around his neck. Closing her lips tightly, she held them against his for a long moment, as she might kiss her nieces.

'And I Belgi, got to *snog-ged* a handsome Frenchman!' Jessica ran her fingers through his hair and studied his open, smiley face with the permanent, itchy, stubble.

I am so going to distract and console you if I have to

The two linked arms again and continued to walk toward the hotel.

'Belgian, Jess. I am from Belgium.'

The following morning the couple ate breakfast of spicy eggs from a *menemen* stall. The dish arrived in a sizzling copper pan and comprised an olive oil stew of tomatoes, onions, chillies and peppers folded through with scrambled eggs and more eggs poached in the juice.

'This is serious hangover scran, even though I hardly had any booze last night. That shit was nice in the water-pipe, not really my bag normally, but what a lovely city to smoke and chill. Probably why I have munchies. The ferryboats look like the Gosport ferries back home in Portsmouth Harbour, let's jump on and see if they go to Gosport. Any news from Netter, or shouldn't I ask? You ok to stay another night? Grand Bazaar later? I've had enough of old buildings and dead people for a bit. Istanbul must stifle in the summer and it is full-on, but I just love it. Do you just love it? And Albay was right about the food, my God. And they spend all their lives eating, why are they not fat? I'm going to order more *menemen,* if you can manage some more? And aren't they all lovely in the city, so fashionable? And the girls are really pretty, I've seen you looking! They are a bit snooty with you men, but I think that's just for show. I know you are with Netter and everything, just for now, but would you like a Turkish girlfriend? Everyone is so friendly until they are behind the wheel. And aren't the cats so pretty, not sure if there aren't too many and I'm not sure who feeds them all? Keeps the mice down, I suppose. Do you like mice?'

Belgi had learned not to try to keep-up with Jessica's chatting. He had taken to her, and she was a good listener, but once she started to talk, it was best to let her get on with it. He nodded and shrugged at the right times, he hoped, his grasp of English only just coping.

They joined a surprisingly efficient scrum to buy return ferry tickets to somewhere and joined another polite scrum to climb aboard one of the ferries moored along the banks of the Bosporus. They had a dry land guard of honour from men in flat caps, women in scarves and teenagers, all holding ridiculously long fishing poles from the banks and the piers of bridges. The Bosporus spewed its cargo of shipping into the Sea of Marmara, and the couple was enthralled by the seeming chaos of life onboard the ferry and the surrounding shipping.

They became aware of tension growing amongst the passengers, followed by a series of public-address announcements from the captain. Before they could ask a fellow passenger for a translation, a bulkhead door opened to the side of the bridge structure and two men in overalls and breathing apparatus appeared in a billow of black smoke, closing the watertight steel door behind them. Within minutes, a frenzy of ferries and smaller boats appeared and circled like sharks. Two ferries came alongside to sandwich the stricken vessel. The engines had clearly shut down and the stricken ferry bobbed uncomfortably in the swell.

Following more shouting and instructions, passengers began to step on to the rescue ferries. There was no obvious panic, everyone helping everyone else. Old people came to the front of the queue, as many willing hands helped the crew disembark the less mobile passengers first. As Jessica and Belgi neared their turn, a young mum or possibly older sister or Au Pair handed a toddler to Jessica and an older child to Belgi, carrying a baby herself. Belgi went first, handing the child to another couple before helping the guardian and then Jessica. The couple and the young family moved away to a quieter part of the boat before the young woman burst into sobs, clutching the children into an uncomfortable hug. Belgi took the little boy back onto his knee and Jessica comforted the young woman, still holding the smaller two.

Within half an hour of breaking free from the stricken ferry, they pulled into the dock of Heybeliada Island, the second of the Princess Islands. The small town was quiet, with just a few tourists browsing the souvenir shops and sitting outside the cafes. The couple took a horse-drawn carriage tour of the island. Belgi, still trembling from the adrenalin rush of the sea rescue, noticed Jessica shudder and brought her closer into a hug. He felt her shoulders heave and as he squeezed her harder, he felt tears stream down his own cheeks.

'Hey, you ok Jess? Do you think we hit an iceberg, I didn't hear the band playing?'

Jessica turned to speak and Belgi saw she was laughing.

'Belgi! That was so exciting. Wasn't that just so much fun?' Seeing his tears, she cupped his face. 'Darling! Don't cry, we are safe and you were so brave.' She pulled him closer to her chest but could not control the laughing. 'Shit, sorry Belgi, it must be hysterics with the adrenalin. I am always being told-off for laughing at the wrong times.'

Soon Belgi joined in laughing between sobs and at that moment, the horse whinnied a laugh, causing the coachman to join-in. As the tour ended, the three people and one horse pulled into the town square, stifling giggles.

Belgi tensed for the ferry trip back to the mainland as Jessica became hyperactive, skipping around deck to take the different views. Back in the city, the couple headed for the Grand Bazaar. Belgi enjoyed the variety and diversity of the stalls, selling everything from hunting rifles and wood stoves to fine silks and gold jewellery. Jessica loved the bedlam and hustle, the beautiful clothes that the Istanbul set wore and the variety of dress from other regions and countries, including the full-length black burka worn by Iranian tourists.

Leaving by a side street dedicated to selling livestock and minibuses, the couple headed back to the hotel for supper. Sitting on the cramped roof terrace just as the sun set over the Blue Mosque, the azan blasted through speakers providing the soundtrack to their raki apéritif.

Jessica drove Belgi back to his campervan, swapped luggage and with Albay's radiogram carefully stowed, headed east for Cappadocia. She did not have the patience or inclination to dawdle behind Belgi, but they agreed to try to meet again in Goreme. The idea of seeing a few people living in caves, in the middle of a hilly, stony Turkish desert did not overly appeal to Jessica. She loved Istanbul, but would try to enjoy the contrasting rustic charm of this backwater, possibly for one night only. She also looked forward to heading to the coast afterward, hopefully to a chic beach resort with some nightlife.

Stopping halfway for a brief sleepover in a dingy *Pansiyon,* the following day Jessica followed a blue campervan into the car park of an impressive stone building, hoping for a café or shop for an early lunch. Two women from the van walked to Jessica, one with blond hair in tight curls and the second with ginger hair and a face full of freckles. Both had naturally fair skin, but even the ginger woman carried a light tan.

'Hey mate! English plates? Long drive.'

The Australian accent sounded thick and friendly.

'Sure. Not all in one go, though. What is this place? I am only really looking for a café.'

'No way, mate. This is where the Whirling Dervishes strut their stuff. You're here now though, so you must come and see. Here, take half of my cheese sanger to see you through. I'm Sheila, and this is Sheila, too. To keep it simple, shall we call you Sheila?'

'Yeah, why not, but the name is Jess. So who and what is this all about?'

The second Sheila spoke. 'Well, they are Sufi Muslims and eight hundred years ago, they discovered if they spin around for a bit, they get closer to God. So, they've been spinning ever since. Bit like taking magic mushies, you know?'

'Sounds .. um .. fascinating. No wait, I mean boring.'

'Yeah Jess, I cannot disagree with you there, it was her idea. She always wanted to be a hippy.' Blond Sheila spoke, gesturing towards her friend who rolled her eyes.

'I thought Sufis lived in Syria, didn't they get chased up a mountain, by IS, recently?'

Both Australians shrugged.

Inside the huge auditorium, a serious-looking young man lectured the audience about the history of Sufism, the Dervishes and the whirling ceremony. He asked the audience not to take photographs, clap, snore or have a good time in any other way. Shortly afterward, a slim man in a felt hat and big white dress walked to the centre of the stage and spun around. After a few minutes he stopped, leaving the stage. Following a short silent delay, five men in felt hats and big white dresses came onto the stage and spun around for a few minutes before leaving the stage. The first man plus another man, possibly one of the five, came onto the stage and spun around for a few minutes. The finale was seven men in felt hats and big white dresses coming onto stage and spinning around for a few minutes, before leaving to no applause, as requested.

Not wanting to appear disrespectful, the audience awaited dismissal. A toddler asked her dad if they could go now; the little girl was a Geordie from Newcastle, so only Jessica and her own parents understood the question. The solemn young man appeared, looking hot and sweaty, with felt-hat-hair, announcing Turkish ice cream and souvenirs were available for purchase in the lobby. Respectfully, the audience filed out.

The three women waited until they were back at their vehicles before speaking. Sheila threw her head back laughing. Sheila Two spoke.

'That wasn't funny Sheila, that was the most pious and mesmerising ceremony I have ever witnessed. Did you appreciate it, Jess?'

'Appreciate it, Sheila? That was the most mind-numbing thing I have ever seen. I will never get those three hours of my life back again!'

'Well, you two, I think you are being unfair and it was less than one hour, actually.' Sheila renewed her laughter as Jessica climbed into the car.

'All I can say is: no wonder rest of the Muslim world finds them irritating. Have you girls been, or are you going, to look at the troglodytes? After that show, I can't wait for the excitement.'

'On our way.' Sheila rummaged in her bag for a hotel card. 'We are going to this hotel, it's recommended, so we will check it out first and move on if no good.' Jessica photographed the card and added the address to her sat-nav.

'Well, I hope it isn't recommended by the same person who suggested the Whirling Dervishes!'

Jessica waited for the Geordie family to pass in front of her car towards the waiting coach, before pulling away. The little girl sucked hard on what looked like warm *ice cream* made of snot and the mother carried a knitted toilet roll cover, in the shape of a Whirling Dervish.

Jessica headed for the hotel recommended by the Australians. She was not interested in meeting-up again and not convinced the recommendation would be solid, but it was somewhere to start. As she drove the road towards Goreme, the landscape became increasingly bleak and alien; mostly desert scrub with rocky outcrops and backed by the distant Taurus Mountains. The land was interspersed with green explosions of heavily irrigated farmland, tiny hamlets and the occasional marble quarry; but the expanses between had a lunar bleakness or at least the appearance of a set from a spaghetti-western.

The road rose over a range of low hills. Jessica turned the bend to descend into the next valley and saw the miles of Cappadocia Fairy Chimneys marching into the distance. She pulled into the side of the road to enjoy the view. Some 'chimney' rock formations close-by were perhaps twenty feet high and stood proudly on the surrounding hillside. The formations stood alone, with the areas between flat and clear, so that

Jessica could walk to one and lean against it for a selfie. Further in the distance, she saw vast ranges of jagged formations, like dragon's teeth. To her right were the strangest formations, with individual chimneys topped with dark caps of rock, which drooped to one side. Jessica could not help but notice the phallic properties of this range. She struggled to guess the dimensions of individual chimneys, but some were at least 100 feet high, around thirty or forty feet in circumference and spaced approximately 100 feet apart. Others she could see sitting in clumps of three or more like mushrooms growing in the tree roots of a giant forest.

Jessica continued to the hotel, walking around the back to an empty terrace and views over a canyon within a valley. Rock chimneys surrounded the hotel and Jessica gave a slight shudder; it felt like being in the set of a science fiction or horror movie, with the countless formations marching slowly towards her. She started at the voice behind her.

'Shit! Don't creep up on me like that. Jesus!'

'Sorry, madam. *Hosgeldiniz.* Welcome to my hotel. Would you like a room, a meal, a drink or just sit please to see the view? I bring you my *Cay,* my gift to a traveller.'

'*Hosbulduk,*' Jessica was keen to use the few phrases she had learned from Albay. 'Tea will be lovely. *Tesekkur ederim.*' Looking towards the closest Fairy Chimney, Jessica pointed to a doorway carved into the side. 'Do you have cave rooms in the hotel?'

'Our hotel has two cave rooms, but they are occupied. We have beautiful stone rooms, you must come this way. Is very modern, more comfortable than cave. More modern. This way, madam.'

Remembering head-shaking shows indecision, Jessica tossed her head in the backward nod of a Turkish no. '*Higher.* My friend wants to stay in a cave. But thank you, *tesekkur ederim.*'

The waiter looked crestfallen. He bowed his head shamefully, touched his heart and, Jessica hoped, went for the tea. The whole terrace area was a mass of floor cushions and low metal tables. Jessica perched on the outside cushion, with the best view of the valley.

To her right, she heard the faint azan call to prayer – crisp with the natural acoustics of the valley. A few seconds later, the next mosque joined in. The two muezzins creating an echo to each other's calls. A few more seconds passed and at the exact time allotted by the official timetable, a third

158

mosque joined in. The call grew louder as the wave of the azan crept closer to the hotel – an unstoppable march of sound, reflected in Jessica's mind by the marching legions of rock formations. At once the mosque closest to the hotel began to call, the minaret speakers at the same level as the hillside terrace where Jessica now stood, clutching the railing. The next mosque began, and then another, further away. The sound bounced along the valley and from side to side, adding to the echoing delay caused by the different start times. The noise hit a crescendo, sending shivers down Jessica's back and causing hairs on her neck and arms to stand on end, as a mass of goosebumps spread across her body. Like a passing locomotive, the valley took the call away from Jessica and further west, as the original muezzins ended their calls and new mosques further away joined in. The whole soundscape lasted just a few minutes; the last calls petered out and Jessica felt her heart slow to normal.

'Your first time here, madam?'

'Shit! Stop doing that. Are you trying to give me a heart attack?'

Jessica turned to see an older man, balding and a little shorter than her, holding an ornate hanging tray with tea, sugar and sweet baklava. 'Sorry, you startled me.'

The man gestured for Jessica to sit as he set her tea onto a low table.

'I am sorry, madam. The azan is most beautiful here. The view is quite biblical and the call to prayer is most impressive.'

'Impressive? My goodness, that is the most powerful and spiritual sound I have ever heard. I was expecting Samson to appear and push asunder a couple of your chimneys! My heart is still pounding. That was awesome, and this place is absolutely magical.'

The man dipped his head with a smile, seemingly taking the credit for everything Jessica admired.

'It is cold and bleak in the winter. It is hot and oppressive in the summer. We have no rain, we are a thousand meters above the sea and the furthest away from the coast of the whole of Turkey. But yes, it is special and close to God.
'My son said you would like a room.' Jessica smiled. He laughed an apology. 'Sorry, I must try.
'You see this cave here? It is a friend's spare guest room. It looks empty, I can ask.'

Jessica followed his finger to a wooden door and window, thirty feet from the ground, up narrow steps cut into the rock face of the closest chimney.

'Wow, yes please, ask. Can you ask for two nights, please? But my friend may stay longer, he will arrive later today.'

The owner met Jessica at the foot of the steps and showed her the room. The *caves* are not natural but hewed from the rock by hand; with the scallop marks, left by the axes, decorating the walls and ceiling. An example of an old axe sat fixed above the door. The owner explained the rock is soft to work under a hard crust. Once work is complete, the air hardens the crust again, making this the easiest rock to work and the most enduring. Except for the doors, window frames and furniture, everything was cut from the rock – wardrobes, window seats, dressing table and the shelf for the coffee machine. The spacious en-suite was modern. The room cost a fraction of the hotel rates.

'Perfect, thank you and so cool.'

'Night-time is cold. Here extra blankets, here electric heater, here spare bed.' The owner pointed to a folding bed under the main double. 'We live below, other side. Is also a market shop, for you. Your husband here soon?' Jessica decided not to complicate the situation and just nodded.

Jessica knew how excited Belgi was to stay in a cave and decided to sleep in the spare bed, giving him the main double, and to decorate the room with flowers and tea lights from the local mini-market. She spent some time exploring the small town and the incredible mix of stone buildings and caves; accommodating the same shops, offices and houses found in any traditional town. She asked the price of a beautiful rug hanging outside a carpet shop, but declined the twenty-thousand-pound price tag. Keen to engage Jessica in conversation, the young man explained how the carpets are used for banking family money, often passing them down the generations or selling one when it was time to build a new house or as dowry for a marrying daughter; a centuries-old form of bitcoin. He brought Jessica tea and showed her a large silk rug coasting eighty-five-thousand-pounds. He was, respectfully, a little flirty and Jessica enjoyed his attention.

For the rest of the afternoon, she relaxed on the hotel terrace, adding to her journal and deciding how long she would stay in Turkey. She loved Gallipoli, Istanbul and now Cappadocia, but decided to spend some time exploring the Aegean

Coast before making more plans. She made a note to travel back west and closed her journal. She also arranged a takeout food delivery for when Belgi arrived.

Back in her cave-room after sunset, Jessica waited for Belgi; following his sat-nav and her road directions from an earlier text. Although it was still early, she treated herself to a long hot shower and dressed in the new silk pyjamas. Then, deciding they were a little too sexy for sharing a room with another woman's boyfriend, she changed again into her warm, white fluffy onesie. The room felt fresh and cool following the heat of the day, and for the first time in weeks, Jessica slipped on a thick pair of hiking socks. She giggled at herself in the mirror and lowered the zip a little, to divert Belgi's eye from her less than flattering outfit.

She heard the familiar tick of the camper's air-cooled engine and rushed to the door, expecting to see Belgi parking his van. Disappointed, she saw the Australian's blue camper arrive. As the two Sheilas returned from reception, Belgi drove in and Jessica watched from the top step, waiting to catch his eye.

Jessica watched as the Australians waited for Belgi, engaging him in conversation seemingly about campervans. Within a few minutes of meeting, Sheila Two found it necessary to touch Belgi's arm. On the second occasion she felt the need to touch his arm, she allowed her hand to rest there as they talked.

Jessica sent a text *'behind you'* and Belgi spun around to see Jessica, giving her an enthusiastic wave, his warm smile clear from across the car park. Grabbing his bag, Belgi quickly abandoned his new friends in favour of Jessica.

'Wow Jessica, this is beautiful. A real cave. Oh my God Jessica, all of these candles, it is beautiful. Thank you.'

'I'm in for the night, Belgi. Are you exploring or are you ok with an evening in? The hotel does takeaways.'

'I would like to sleep with you, Jess. I mean, I am exhausted after my journey and I like to stay in, with you and sleep early.' Jessica wrinkled her nose and smiled at his Freudian slip, but he showed no obvious sign of embarrassment.

Belgi showered as Jessica laid the stone table and uncovered the cold meze starters. Once he sat, she texted the hotel to confirm the main course.

'Man, you will not believe how wonderful this place is in daylight. I have arranged a guide tomorrow but say if you do not fancy. This room is private, but the hotel is so helpful and I have a big surprise for you tomorrow. I see you met the Sheilas, aren't they both pretty? Sheila Two is cute, but too many freckles for my liking, have you spoken with Netter? You can rent the room for longer if you want; I am heading for the coast, were you ok driving in Turkey on your own? I've seen the Whirling Dervishes, but, you know, you'd have to want to.'

Belgi waited for his turn to speak and they talked about their day.

'Netter has not called. Maybe not calling. But I will stay here in a cave for a week before heading home.'

Jessica saw Belgi coping perfectly well with the Netter situation, but not one to miss an opportunity, she leaned across the table, cupped his face and kissed his forehead.

'We have each other, Belgi.'

Jessica realised how lame her response sounded, but if Belgi needed any consoling, it would not be by Sheila Two.

The waiter knocked and entered the room carrying a tray with two plates of peppers, onions, boiled potatoes and rice. Placing them on the table with bread, he also set down two hot clay pots, sealed closed with a lid of clay.

'Tesekur ederim. Cok hos. Ama nasil?' Jessica had practiced the first part of her Turkish phrase in her head, ready to impress Belgi. She had not expected to have to ask 'But how?' to the waiter and so tipped her hands upwards to ensure he understood the question. In any event, she had impressed Belgi.

'This is lamb, Belgi, but I'm not sure how you open the pot.'

The waiter smiled. 'Is lamb in oven. Is best lamb you ever taste. No air, no burn. Is Sultan's lamb. Also paprika, onion, apricot, some chillies, some peppers.'

Taking a serving spoon from his apron pocket, the waiter leaned over Belgi and tapped the top of the pot until it shattered into several large pieces; removing the broken pottery with the spoon. Jessica followed suit with her own. The smell of the spicy lamb immediately filled the room as Belgi shifted in his seat in anticipation.

'Afiyet Olsun.'

'Sensationnel! This is the best lamb ever, Jessica. Beautiful.' He spoke the last word looking directly into Jessica's eyes. Her grin widened with pride. 'Beautiful, Jess. Can I ask, it is not a problem, just of interest – we have half a lamb each here and with starters - can I ask how much our banquet has cost tonight? My treat, I insist.'

Jessica gestured towards the travel memoir, When In Roam, on the window seat.

'Well, it was a little more than the cost of Pamdiana Jones' white rice every day, but she would still be proud of me. Four-pounds each for all the food and around the same for the wine.' Jessica could see she had impressed Belgi with her efforts to make his cave experience extra special.

She explained the sleeping arrangements and Belgi agreed on the understanding that he picked-up the room tab. Eventually, they struck a complicated deal of who was to pay for what over the coming days. While Belgi used the bathroom, Jessica climbed into her folding bed and adjusted the mirror on her shelf; turning away from Belgi but spying on him strip down to his shorts in the mirror. She decided he was no Jason Taylor from the Cinque Terre, but she would still enjoy comforting him later, if necessary. She almost

167

hoped Netter would call tonight, but then she pushed the thought to the back of her head.

Jessica crept from the room to leave Belgi sleeping and joined the Australians on the hotel floor cushions for morning coffee.

'I thought you were travelling alone, mate?'

'I am Sheila. Just friends.'

'Cosy.' Sheila Two added. 'So Belgi is single then?'

'No, he isn't, actually. He is dating a girl and we are expecting to catch-up with her soon. She is my friend.'

Sheila Two spoke to Jessica, but looked at her friend with a grin.

'So how long have I got mate?'

'You have no time, Sheila. Dating, friend – what part of those two words are you struggling with, exactly?' Jessica removed all emotion from her voice.

'Hey, easy mate! I am not asking your permission here.'

Sheila squeezed her friend's arm.

'Easy Sheila, you heard what Jess said.'

Sheila Two glared at Jessica and then at her friend. Before she could escalate the disagreement further, the three women saw Belgi make his way down the cave steps and towards the terrace. Sheila Two quickly cleared the floor cushions next to her and plumped scatter cushions to make a nest for Belgi.

'Ladies, may I join you and enjoy the view, please?'

Belgi stood with his back to the scenery and purposely looked at Sheila Two with a cheeky grin. He smelt the coffee and stepped over the legs of the Australians, as Sheila Two patted the cushion for him to sit. Belgi took another two strides and flopped next to Jessica. With his arm around her neck, he pulled her closer to kiss the top of her head.

'Jess, thanks again for last night. It was the best I have ever had, honest. And I think you liked it also? That pot of lam…' Jessica raised a finger to his lips.

'I did my love and thank you for treating me.'

Jessica leaned forward slightly to ensure the Sheilas could see her smug smile. Jessica heard the call to prayer from far away to the east end of the valley.

'Come here Belgi.' Jessica pulled Belgi to his feet and walked him to the railing. 'Just listen.'

As the tsunami of calls, counter calls and echoes washed down the valley and over the couple, Belgi straightened and shuddered. The biblical sound, in this biblical stone landscape, sent shivers down his spine. Jessica rubbed his back.

'Oh my God Jessica, this is your surprise? I wish Netter is here with us, to hear this.' Jessica saw his eyes moisten and she squeezed his arm.

As the couple returned to their shared cushion, Jessica decided to regain the adult high ground from the Sheilas.

'Who are you texting there, Sheila Two? Do you ever get homesick?'

'Not really mate, not when I travel with Sheila here, but thanks for asking. I'm texting a pom we met, but I don't think it is going anywhere. What does he mean here in this text - I'm a "marmite-moment" girl?'

'Well, marmite is like vegemite, a yeast extract. Isn't that right, Jess?' offered Sheila.

'Yeah, it is. Did you give him a yeast infection or something?'

Sheila and Belgi widened their eyes at Jessica's rudeness, and even Jessica realised she had gone too far.

'No mate, I fucking did not. Why would you say that?'

Jessica smiled and began back peddling. Belgi and Sheila looked down to avoid involvement. Belgi tensed a little, ready to intervene in any fight, and Sheila did the same.

'Or it can mean that you either love something or hate something – no middle ground. It isn't meant as an insult.'

'I didn't say he insulted me, mate.'

Jessica shrugged. Trying again, she added, 'Here girls, can you read? I mean do you read, sorry, obviously you probably *can* read.'

Belgi giggled almost silently, watching Jessica dig this hole deeper. Now both Australians glared at Jessica.

'Um, it's just that I thought you might like this to read. It is so funny and has a bit about Australia and I've finished reading it.' Jessica pulled her copy of When In Roam from her bag, ripping the front cover in half. 'Shit! That's a brilliant cover of Pam Jones bungee jumping.'

Jessica held up the peace offering - ripped, well-thumbed and looking past its best. Belgi laughed louder; neither Australian moved to take the book.

'So what's so fucking funny with you, frog? Taking the piss?' Sheila Two spoke in a growl.

Belgi buried his face into his hands, trying to stifle his laughter and shaking his head.

'No sorry, I laugh at her.' He pointed at Jessica.

Shelia opened her bag.

'Thanks for the book mate, cheers. I'll swap it for this book, Max Speed's, Lads Reunited. Your mate there will love it, hilarious right from the very first line. Real English humour.
'Look guys, I think we are divided by a common language here, lets restart. Yeah?'

The other two women nodded as Belgi continued to laugh. Jessica rose to use the bathroom and as she stepped over the Sheilas' legs, Sheila Two spoke.

'Hey mate, have you any Durex in that bag, or can you ask at reception please?' Jessica stared down at the Australian. 'Now what have I done, mate? You just have it in for me!'

Jessica's neck muscles tightened and her breathing deepened. 'He was just talking about his girlfriend. Leave, him, the, fuck, alone!'

'Ok mate. I don't want his babies – I only asked for some Durex!'

Sheila Two flipped on to her feet, much quicker and more agile than Jessica expected. Jessica stood a couple of inches taller and held her ground, looking down slightly into the other's face.

'I'll ask reception myself mate, no worries.'

Jessica pushed past and on to the restrooms. When she had finished, she splashed water onto her face, taking deep breaths to calm herself. Returning to the terrace, she saw Sheila Two repairing the book cover with a reel of sticky tape. Inside the reel was the manufacturer's name printed repeatedly in a spiral – *'Durex'*.

'Shit! Durex tape – Sellotape! Sorry, Sheila Two, I am so sorry, I misunderstood.'

'I don't care about the brand mate, so long as it's sticky. Sheila had some in her bag. You need to chill, mate!'

Belgi renewed laughing. In a perfect Sid James impersonation, he added, 'Behind every angry woman, stands a man who has absolutely no idea what he did wrong!' Only Sheila laughed.

The guide they arranged doubled as the waiter from the hotel. The Australians booked on to the same tour and to save the cost of the guide hiring a minibus, offered to drive everyone in their campervan. Sheila drove, Waiter rode shotgun, and Sheila Two climbed into the back of the camper. Jessica deliberately took the seat next to Sheila Two, forcing Belgi to sit on the floor, away from his new admirer. Jessica wrapped one leg across his chest to stake her claim.

Waiter spoke of how the area was originally blanketed in volcanic rock. The softer rock underneath then eroded away in the badlands and drainage valleys, to leave the towering pillars of soft rock protected and capped with the harder black volcanic rock.

'So how come you know all this stuff, Waiter?' Shelia asked from the driving seat.

'I am waiter to earn wage. But I also archaeologist. I have mastered and now working on PhD. I have degree in Middle-Eastern Political and Religious History and a diploma in the study of local flora and fauna. You must ask me anything.'

'Strewth – I'd be happy to understand all those words you just used!'

'People live here two-thousand years before Jesus born, in Bronze Age. Talking of Jesus, this is where idea of Christian Trinity developed. If not for my ancestors, you only have Father and Son. No Holy Ghost.'

Belgi spoke 'Christians here, in Turkey?'

'Of course. Mary lived in Turkey after her son's crucifixion. Paul the Apostle lived in Efes. Early hagiographies from Cappadocian Fathers. They interpreted original sin for Christianity and invented feminine virtue.'

'Well, thanks for that one.' Jessica offered. 'And we've been subjugated by you Abrahamics ever since!'

'You started it.' Waiter replied matter-of-factly. Jessica raised her eyebrows and Waiter clarified. 'You gave Adam the apple!'

'The Catholic Church?' Belgi asked, before Jessica could engage Waiter further.

'Earlier than Roman times. Early Orthodox – before you paganised Christianity.'

They parked the camper and walked into a splash of green vegetation in an otherwise stone and arid environment. They hiked valleys full of cave and stone churches, ancient rock-carved pigeon lofts for collecting guano, onyx mines, lunar landscapes of ash and tuff from the Neocene period.

At a remote village, they stopped for *Sac Tava*, a fried spicy minced-lamb dish, and Jessica bought a beautifully crafted but childishly simple rag doll.

'Very sad story. This doll only made in this village. A long time ago, a lady's baby die. She make herself a baby from rags. I think she mad, very sad. Now all women here make the dolls.'

'Perhaps all women are mad, Waiter. Very sad.' Belgi offered helpfully; careful to avoid looking at Sheila Two and Jessica.

They drove to the start of the next valley.

176

'This we call Love Valley.' The chimneys soared above them, each pillar of rock capped with a black tip.

'Why love valley?' Sheila Two asked.

Her four companions stared at her, Belgi with his cheeky grin. Waiter scrutinised the 130-foot phallus soaring above them, and the range of phalluses disappearing into the distance.

'Ah, maybe I am not sure, lady. Perhaps they not explain me at *universite.*'

'Strewth Sheila! There are a thousand 30m rock dildos in front of you – keep-up mate!'

Waiter stopped to point out each new plant, camouflaged bird and lizard, until they reached a shed standing guard over a hole in the cliff face. They paid £2 each at the shed to enter the hole. Jessica followed Waiter with Belgi and then the Sheilas following behind. Inside the hole, Waiter headed down a flight of stone steps, illuminated by a string of electric lamps. He stopped where the steps widened, turned and spoke to his party. Jessica noticed Shelia Two had grabbed Belgi's hand for comfort in the dark.

'This underground city. Was home to twenty-thousand people, the entire town. It has religious

177

school, stable, stalls for livestock, presses for fruit and wine cellars, stores, living places, bathhouse. Is underground sixty meters. Every floor has Indiana-Jones-style stone doors. Full-size cruciform church. I show you everything, but sometimes is too narrow to stop and talk.'

Jessica spoke. 'How did they breathe down here?'

'Also this, is fifty-five-meter long ventilation shaft, hidden on surface, to church on level five; also to send water to surface for people outside or down for people inside, like a Stupid-Waiter.'

'Dumb-Waiter. So who were they hiding from?'

'Maybe hundreds of years before Jesus born. Perhaps to escape other towns liking to attack and also from scorching sun and cold snow. Always same pleasant temperature here, underground. Then to hide from Arabs during Byzantine wars. Then Mongolian Hoards. From Byzantine time, these people are Christian – they even hide from Ottomans, until First World War. When Turks take area, they hide from Greek invaders.'

'And the enemy never found them?' Belgi asked.

'Never. After Turkish Republic, we forgot where the underground cities are until a local person found a tunnel in 1968. Last year, we find another city, bigger than this. Underground is others, maybe forty, maybe hundred, connected by tunnels, so they could still visit and trade underground. I show you, follow me, and careful your stepping.'

As Belgi took a step forward, Jessica eased herself between him and Sheila Two.

'Sorry, love. I didn't see you there in the dark.'

Sheila Two tightened her hold on Belgi's hand and the three progressed slowly down the passage cramped together, Sheila repeatedly stepping on Jessica's heels and Jessica on Belgi's. Eventually, Jessica stopped the procession and gripping Belgi's and Sheila Two's wrists, prised them apart. With insufficient room and light for Belgi to work out what was happening behind him, he could only feel the confusion of hands and the pulling of his, before an Australian accent pierced the darkness.

'Fuck sake, you pommie bitch.'

Followed by a calmer Australian accent further back.

'Hey Sheila, walk here, with me.'

The group completed the tour through passages, rooms and steep steps, eventually bursting back into the blinding light at the surface. Sheila drove back, Waiter rode shotgun and Belgi leaned forward, talking about the wonders of their tour. Jessica and Sheila Two sat in stony silence, staring at each other.

Jessica asked to pull over at the carpet shop and pushed Belgi out of the van, saying goodbye to the others as she followed. She introduced Belgi to the shop owner, and the three drank tea and discussed the day's adventure – Jessica showing Belgi the silk carpet from her previous visit. They walked back to the room through dark stone streets, lit by a few glows leaking from the windows of stone houses and caves, and the moon.

'Do you fancy Sheila Two, Belgi? I think she is a bit obvious, you know, tarty and common. Don't you think? And dead needy. Did you smell her in the donkey stable, underground? I wouldn't trust her. I thought she was a dyke at first. Do you like Australians? I like the other Sheila, but I'm not sure about Sheila Two. I don't think she will age well. Big bones, I wonder if her parents are fat. She's too skinny at the moment but that won't last. I wonder what she does for work, or do you think she is on welfare?'

'Hey Jessica, please. She is lovely, I like her. She is cute and clever.' Jessica pouted and chewed her bottom lip. 'But I am seeing Netter. And I hope you are not jealous.'

'Jealous! Me! Of you and the skinny-fat bitch? Don't flatter yourself Belgi!'

Belgi snorted a giggle as they continued towards their room.

'So it doesn't matter that I think you are prettier, even when you dress like a polar bear with socks, for bed?'

Jessica looked up from the road and smiled. 'Yes I am prettier, Belgi. Thank you. And Netter is prettier than both Sheilas.'

'Yes. Did I say she phone?'

'No, you didn't say! When? What did she say? Christ Belgi!'

'Sorry, I forgot. This morning. Phone woke me. She miss me. She think I am worth knowing better. I make her laugh. I go to Ankara station in four days, for her. Driving is ok.'

They stepped into the glow of a window. Jessica spun Belgi around to face her. His grin was as wide as her own.

Belgi could see his friend was pleased for him and so wondered why her long sigh sounded disappointed.

Jessica and Belgi hugged at the car.

'Belgi, you are lovely, you could have any girlfriend – laughter is the best aphrodisiac…'

'Max Speed must get lucky then, Lads Reunited is such a funny book, I laugh at every line. I will keep it for you to read if we meet again.'

'Belgi, shush sweetheart, you interrupted me. Just listen and let us not allow your Max Speed to ruin this moment. Now, the guy in the carpet shop has my mobile number. So does your landlord, Waiter and hotel owner. My spies are everywhere. Never underestimate my ability to find shit out. I even know you dreamt about me last night, I liked the way you tugged my hair!'

The couple laughed together and Belgi made no effort to deny the accusation.

'So, if you hook-up with Sheila Two or any girl, I will know. And I will tell Netter. And I will cut your bollocks off, with a… with a rusty spoon. Shall I translate any of that into French, or are we cool?' Jessica smiled sweetly at her friend.

'Cool, Jessica, thank you. The most dangerous animal in the world is a smiling woman, especially one with a rusty spoon.'

'Give Netter my love; lucky cow.'

Jessica headed west towards the coast, spending a day exploring the ruins of the Roman City Ephesus, complete with a towering library, amphitheatre and preserved town toilets. Once a port town, it now sat ten miles from the sea. In the evening, she relaxed in the thermal waters of Pamukkale, *Cotton Castle Mountain* - swimming amongst Roman pillars in the Antique pool and bathing in the shallow, shimmering, snow-white travertine terraces. As she prepared to leave early on the following morning, the sky filled with hot air balloons, a handful of which touched-down around her.

The captain of the closest balloon called to Jessica, waving her over. She rushed to the balloon and clambered into the basket just as it ascended. Except for the occasional burst of gas, the party in the balloon glided silently, high above Pamukkale and the Holy Roman City of Hierapolis. None of the Turkish passengers spoke English, and so Jessica was excluded from any debate. She watched the sun rise over the horizon

184

of the plain and white *Cotton Castle Mountain* burst into reflected shades of red and gold.

She continued her road trip west to the coast and then south through pretty, cobbled villages, bustling towns and beach resorts. With nowhere particular in mind, she headed in the vague direction of Marmaris and Bodrum; familiar names of tourist towns. Drifting inland by accident, Jessica spent one night in the regional capital of Mugla, finding a room in the old Ottoman quarter and visiting the town's seven-hundred-year-old *Hanam* Turkish Baths.

She relaxed on the hot marble bench, jugging hot water over herself from the running faucets and watching a hen party of girls and women chatting, splashing each other and washing. A young woman entered wearing a yellow Lycra vest and shorts. She beckoned Jessica to the marble slab, positioned like a sacrifice alter in the middle of the sauna. Jessica felt self-conscious walking to the middle wearing only a thin wet towel around her waist; she caught the attention of the hen party.

'Lie Lady! On front.'

The masseur tugged off Jessica's towel as she climbed onto the slab and folded it over her bottom. Gently, she rubbed a soapy pillowcase-shaped cloth the length of Jessica's body, from the very top of her head to the bottom of her feet, rinsing and soaping the cloth as she went. Turning Jessica onto her back, she repeated the gentle rub over Jessica's front-half, finishing by pouring jugs of hot water to rinse away the suds and crud, which had accumulated over the previous days.

The masseur rested her hand on Jessica's chest to prevent her from standing; there was more to come. The hen party giggled. Masseur flipped the pillowcase to puff it into a soapy fabric balloon and scrubbed Jessica's head, face and body; this part of the process was less gentle. Jessica flinched and giggled as the pillowcase scrubbed into every corner and crevice of her body. The more Jessica giggled and spluttered, the more the hens laughed at the writhing mass of bubbles on the slab. Rolls of dead skin surrounded her and more gallons of hot water rinsed everything away.

Masseur wiped Jessica all over with the damp cloth, before massaging oil into her skin. As she worked, Masseur kneaded her hands and fists deep into Jessica's muscles. Using the heel of her hand, she worked along the length of Jessica's legs and back, digging thumbs into the soles of her feet. Taking each limb and shoulders in turn, she contorted Jessica's body painfully into impossible shapes; joints cracked and gristle crackled. Eventually, she stood at the top end of Jessica, gently massaging her head, temples and face.

Helping Jessica stand and wrapping a thin dry towel around her waist, she guided her out of the sauna to the clapping and goodbyes of the hens, and into a dry room full of fluffy towels and laundered dressing gowns, and then on to an area of sofas and fruit drinks. Back in her hotel room Jessica fell asleep, sat up in bed with her journal open across her lap.

Jessica set off early again, enjoying the fresh cool morning air and empty roads. An hour outside of Mugla, she zigzagged down a mountain road with vistas of the impossibly turquoise Aegean Sea. She pulled off the trunk road into a village signposted Koyaka and parked in front of a Bed and Breakfast.

Jessica spent an hour walking along the river path past fish restaurants and along the empty, narrow sand beach, to a eucalyptus forest; returning through the village of whitewashed houses with ornate wooden balconies and pitched tile roofs. This was truly a fairytale village. The men she passed respectfully nodded, and the women beamed smiles and waved. She returned *hosbulduk* to the welcoming *hosgeldiniz* greetings. Jessica had found the place to settle until her holiday visa expired.

Jessica returned to the car and about to enter the Bed-and-Breakfast for a room, noticed the shack shaded below eucalyptus trees by the river. The roof caught a smattering of leaves and nuts across the corrugated iron, but the building appeared well maintained and recently painted. A hand-painted *Satilik* sign with a phone number hung on the wall. Jessica walked around the outside of the shack, pushing open the unlocked door and checking the one bedsit room with a separate bathroom. The shack contained minimal furniture; dustsheets covered everything and utilities were all switched off. She closed the door behind her and sat on a log at the side of the crystal-clear river.

It took only a moment to decide. Jessica dialled the number.

'Hello. Speak English?'

'No. Little.'

'Your house? Near river?'

'Evet. You want?'

'Yes. For three months. For summer.'

'Evet. No problem. Is yours. Thank you. Goodbye.'

The line died. Jessica began to type a text, keeping the sentences short and avoiding anything complicated that could be misunderstood. Before she had finished, a flatbed van stopped on the edge of the road. It was sign painted and had loose building materials in the back. A smiling middle-aged couple stepped out.

'English lady? Phone? *Hosgeldiniz'*

'Hosbulduk. Is this your house? Can I rent for three months please, how much?'

'*Evet.* Is yours. Is one thousand pounds and five hundred pounds.'

'For how long?'

'*Evet.'*

'One thousand five hundred British Pounds for three months?'

'Evet. For long time. Is now yours.'

The man extended his arm and Jessica shook hands. 'Ok, deal! *Tammam.'*

The woman beamed a smile at Jessica and unloaded cleaning products and brushes from the van, before cleaning the inside of the house. The man used rakes and brooms to clean the small wooden veranda and a strip of gritty dirt. They swung open the shutters, turned on the electricity, lit the gas fridge and showed Jessica around.

'Is no drain. This is drain.' He pointed to a tank outside of the bathroom.

'No electricity. This electricity.' The man pointed to a tiny wind turbine spinning in the sea breeze. 'Is battery here.'

'No water. This water.' He took Jessica by the wrist, pointing to a garden hose pinned to the outside wall and disappearing into the roof space. He then guided her along an imaginary line, pointing to the ground. Fifty yards further on, they crossed a dirt track and stopped at the hillside. He pointed to the hose appearing from under the track and snaking up the steep hill. Forty-feet above the road, the hose ended with a funnel pinned to the hillside in the flow of a fast stream. 'Here water.'

'No land. Only house. Understand? No build new house. Understand?'

'Yes, I think so. And it is my house for three months, for the summer? Then I go home to England.'

'Yes, your house now.'

The woman produced documents from the van, and the three sat at a picnic table.

'Sign here. And here and here. No tax number? I fix. And here. Passport number. And here. And name. And here, for army. And here for council. And here.' Jessica read the final and only paragraph in English.

This document has been translated by a government-approved translator and I fully understand the contents.

Jessica signed.

'Is your house now, I am *temsil yetkisi*. Understand? I am *Muhtar*. Understand?'

'You are the owner? You are Muhtar? I am Jessica.'

'*Evet.* Sign here and here. My shop here.' Muhtar pointed to the van signwriting and then into the distance along the road. 'You have money please?'

'No, not on me. Can I transfer?' Jessica waved a credit card. The couple laughed.

'Money tomorrow, or another day. No problem. *Gorusuruz.*'

The couple collected the documents and drove away, waving.

Jessica enjoyed making the house a home, adding a few hooks for clothes and pinning throws to the walls for decoration. She also enjoyed cooking properly for the first time since leaving England and became friendly with the locals, waiters and shopkeepers. She transferred the rent to her pre-charge card and then cashed the money as euros at the post office. Muhtar counted the money twice, checked the exchange rate and gave her twenty euros, in change.

The days were warm and the nights cool enough to sleep with the 12V desk fan. She posted photographs of herself and the shack on Facebook and to family and friends. She sent a smiling photograph of herself to Chris without an accompanying message, and he returned three kisses with a smiley emoji. Jessica sent a message to Netter and Belgi – no promises, but they were planning to visit Ephesus and would drop by to see Jessica, if possible.

The council visited, checking she had not erected a fence or out-buildings to her short let. The Jandarma visited to check her passport. The officer was a little aloof, but the two soldiers that came with him were all smiles, guns and uniforms. Jessica felt most satisfied following the visit.

Jessica also befriended a ten-year-old boy who would visit on the way to and from school, running errands and translating for her. He accepted only an occasional coin for his services and if Jessica required no errands, he would spend half an hour sitting on her tiny veranda or swimming in the river wearing just his school Y-fronts.

'I am Oglan. I speak perfect English. My father is Muhtar. I show you my library, my butcher and my tailor.'

'You have a library in this tiny village?'

'No. I take you where you want to go. Stay here lady, I show you my dog.'

Walking to the road opposite the Bed-and-Breakfast, Oglan whistled and shouted.

'Uysal! Uysal! *Gel!'*

Jessica watched as the local pack of mostly docile stray dogs shifted in their patches of shade, come together and begin yapping.

'Uysal! *Gel! Yemek!'*

Seconds later, a huge tan Anatolian Shepherd Dog came into view, trotting down the centre of the road. It had a strange gait, running at an angle and turning his head from side to side. The local strays grew agitated as Uysal trotted closer. He moved to the side of the road to avoid the local pack, but as he came into their territory, two dogs peeled off and attacked him – the others barking support. One aggressor made for his head as the other snapped at his hindquarters. Uysal twisted to defend himself and Oglan joined the fray – shouting, waving his arms and kicking out at the strays. Uysal broke free and restarted his trot, Oglan running by his side.

Jessica recoiled at the sudden dogfight and felt nervous as Uysal drew closer. The dog looked at least sixty kilograms, possibly more. Tail wagging, Uysal ran on to the veranda and flopped onto his back at Jessica's feet, pushing her backward so that she stumbled against the shack. He twitched his lips into a one-sided snarl – an Elvis smile. Jessica fell in love.

'Is my dog. Now is your dog also. He likes you. Very gentle. His name is Uysal, he is very obedient, but he will not do what you tell him. I think he is stupid, perhaps. He is blind in this eye.'

Jessica had bought foils of food to feed a couple of the scrawny cats that lived on the roof of the shack and under the wood store away from the sun. She fetched one for Elvis.

'Sorry, Oglan, I cannot look after him. You must take him home. Sorry.'

'He is too old to live on the street. He is ten, his birthday is my birthday. He is my friend as baby. You should not have fed him lady, he goes nowhere now. You will be happy together.'

Oglan collected his schoolbooks and waved goodbye. Jessica knelt beside Elvis and forced her hand into the fleece of his coat. She could not penetrate the thick pile to his skin and so heaved a handful of fur from side to side in way of petting the dog. He turned to face his good eye towards Jessica and snarled his lopsided smile.

'Welcome home, Elvis.'

Occasionally people wandered through Jessica's garden, especially when strolling along the riverbank. Jessica was unsure of the protocol but this casual trespass happened with good humour; Jessica wondered if there was a right-of-way. On this occasion a Jandarma sergeant passed. Seeing Jessica sat on her veranda, he straightened, saluted and smiled. Jessica returned the smile. His uniform was darker than the previous soldiers she had seen. The boots polished to a high gloss. He wore a black bomber jacket in place of the usual hi-vis. He was tall, broad and, Jessica decided, really quite attractive.

'Another visit? Checking I haven't erected a fence or a block of flats?'

'Good morning, *bayan.* I am just strolling. I have an hour to use, before reporting to barracks. I am looking for a morning coffee.'

'Then you have found it. Please sit. My name is Jess. I recognise you, we have met before.'

Jessica took the opportunity to study the visitor. His high-laced boots. His black uniform, the gun belt and holster, complete with semiautomatic pistol, a Turkish flag printed on to the butt of the ammunition clip. The handcuffs in the leather pouch. The blue, red and black tunic showing from under the bomber jacket, covering his muscular chest and bulging arms. The beautiful face, open, friendly, chiselled. Jessica imagined pressing her nose against his chest and smelling the heavy cotton and leather of his uniform. She might smell the gun oil. The soldier's cologne, mixed with the combination of soap and fresh musk.

'*Bayan?*'

'Sorry.' Jessica's voice squeaked. Her attention elsewhere and her mouth dry from breathing with her jaw dropped open. In an effort to clear her throat and wet her lips at the same time, she almost swallowed her tongue. 'I. I am… I am sure we have met.'

'I do not think so, madam. I am from Istanbul.'

'Beautiful. Istanbul, I mean. Istanbul is beautiful. Please call me Jess.'

'My name is Cavus. Friends call me Chav. Also beautiful.' The soldier continued to look at Jessica.

'Thank you. I like Cavus. In England, Chav means… ' *I could just call you sir*

Jessica gestured to her hiking shorts and the more modest of her bikini tops she wore.

'Thank you, but this? Phaa! I do not feel beautiful, but it is nice of you to say so.'

The soldier had a soft, tinkling laugh; it reminded Jessica of someone she knew. Her heart missed a beat.

'You are indeed beautiful, Jess. But I actually meant Koyaka is beautiful, like Istanbul.'

'Yes. I knew that. Look, please sit. I will fetch coffee. I just need to bring it out from the kitchen. Boil the kettle first. Oh, and buy some coffee, I've run out.' The soldier's laugh tinkled again.

'Or tea? Water, perhaps. If easier, Jess.'

'Tea. Of course. Tomorrow you must stop by again, for coffee.'

'Ok, a date.'

'A date! Really? A date? Wow, ok. Yes, why not? A date.'

The soldier laughed again and took his seat. Jessica appeared from the shack with a glass pot of tea and tulip glasses.

'I am on holiday, for two weeks. We are ordered to wear uniform when travelling, for the moment. Show a presence, with everything that is going on in the country and on our borders. I shall sign in my weapons and some uniform to the local barracks. I can stay in the barracks, but I would like a pleasant room somewhere instead, for my holiday, more private. Perhaps the Bed-and-Breakfast behind you. Can you recommend?'

'Yes, Cavus. I definitely recommend that you sleep here. Not right here!' Jessica laughed and blushed. 'Obviously. What must you think of me? I just have the one bed. It is…' Jessica's response sounding more of an invitation than a refusal. 'But the Bed-and-Breakfast is really nice. Lovely owner. Yes, I recommend that you stay. Why is your uniform so, black?'

Cavus poured more tea.

'My uniform is from JOH. Part of Jandarma, but not policing. Different.'

Oglan walked into view carrying one end of a sea kayak, a school friend at the other end. Elvis trotted next to him, swaying his head from side to side. The procession stopped and stared at the visitor. Elvis gave a low, rumbling growl, his heckles raised.

'Hey lady. You want to buy? For only hundred and fifty pounds. I can fix damage with this.' Oglan held up a pot of body fillcr. 'It has engine also. My friend will sell in market tomorrow, if you do not want.' The boy's eyes did not leave Cavus. 'When you go back to England, my friend will sell in market for you. Or you can give it to me.'

'Oglan! That is lovely, thank you and yes, please. We will use it together and you can also go out with your friend if your mother agrees. Thank you so much. Can I give you the money, when shall we fix it? Shall we paint it a new colour?'

Oglan and his friend lowered the kayak to the ground and backed towards the road.

'Is ok lady. Later, after school.'

Elvis lay in the dust under the shadow of the kayak and continued his growl. Jessica looked at Cavus.

'It is ok, Jess. I am a stranger to the children and the dog. They are nervous. Especially with the uniform, I must look very odd to them.'

'Well, I think you look gorgeous.'

'Sorry, Jess?'

Shit! I said that aloud.

Cavus appeared again the following morning, as promised. Jessica had already prepared the table with coffee cups, croissants warm from the oven, and jam. She wore her more daring bikini top and a new pair of long baggy shorts that gathered above her knee. The shorts had a striking, colourful, oriental design, the thin material billowing in the breeze. Once Cavus sat, she fetched the cafeteria. Approaching the table from the southeast, she ensured the low morning sun penetrated the thin cotton shorts and backlit her shape. Cavus noticed.

'You have a lovely spot here Jess.' Cavus unzipped his bomber jacket, identical to his uniform jacket, but with all insignia missing. He wore a white T-shirt and a long pair of grey surfer shorts.

'Shorts and a coat? Very summery.'

Cavus opened the front of his jacket to reveal a pistol in a high holster. He wore a webbing belt against his skin to hold the holster.

'It is a nuisance. My friends at the barracks will find me a reinforced satchel today, which I can tether in my hotel room. My other weapon I have handed in, but I must have this one – available.'

'*Other weapon*? You have a rocket launcher or something?'

Cavus shook his head. 'Just my pistol you saw yesterday. This smaller pistol is for personal protection, only. It is very irritating. No swimming for me today.'

Jessica felt her heart pound. She could see the butt of the pistol and the shape of handcuffs folded into a clip on the holster.

'Can I, you know, hold it?'

'That is probably not permitted Jess, sorry. And why would you want to, is this a kinky thing?'

Cavus laughed, gently teasing Jessica. She smiled; he watched her nose crinkle as she held his eye.

'Yeah. Kinda. Nobody thinks it strange for a boy to be interested in guns, but everyone thinks it is odd for a girl. I like all things – uniform, military. My sister thinks I am a freak and I have an early memory of mum telling me off for asking dad *exactly* what he got up to on deployment. Perhaps I should have been a government assassin or something instead of flogging warships!' Jessica shrugged, keeping her smile.

Cavus folded his arm across his chest, resting his hand on the pistol through the jacket. He spent several seconds looking around.

'May I see the inside of your house? Only if that is appropriate, I don't want to compromise your… reputation.'

Jessica snorted a giggle.

'You are a bit late for that Cavus – I have spent my entire adult life *compromising my reputation* and enjoying every minute of it.'

She leaned over the table placing her hands onto his waist, sliding one hand under his and on to the bulge in his jacket. Lowering her face against his but stopping just short of a kiss, she whispered.

'Walk this way, soldier boy.'

Cavus kicked off his beach shoes as he entered the shack. He walked the length of the single reception and opened the bathroom door, noting the small high window. He reached the shutter and pulled it closed. Walking back into the main room, he scanned the open windows with net screens and billowing curtains - seemingly satisfied that he had those covered. He slipped off his jacket and threw it onto the bed, which Jessica made-up as a day lounger covered in scatter cushions. He placed his hands on his hips, so as not to obscure the pistol. Jessica gulped, her eyes wide.

'You have keys for the handcuffs?'

Cavus nodded, Jessica saw a key fastened to the holster clip. Using both hands, she tugged the handcuffs free and moved to fasten one to Cavus' wrist.

'No way Jess, sorry.' He took the handcuff from her and fastened it loosely around her wrist, smiling. She cleared her throat, licked her lips and squeezed the handcuff tight – the second shackle left hanging, open.

Jessica stroked the butt of the pistol and the length of the snub holster, flicking a leather popper that secured the gun. She rested her hand on the butt and looked-up into Cavus' face, blinking. Slowly she eased the gun from the holster, watching Cavus. She expected him to intervene at any moment.

'Loaded?'

'Of course.'

She now held the pistol flat in both hands. She ran a finger gently along the trigger, her hand trembling. Raising the pistol to her face, Jessica smelled the oil. Running her tongue along the barrel, she could taste the cold metal twang with the sweetness of the oil. She was about to slip the barrel into her mouth when Cavus gently took it away. She gave an involuntary pout. Smiling at her, Cavus flicked a switch to release the ammunition clip, slipping the magazine into his shorts pocket. Jessica started and took a step backward, as Cavus snapped back the slide checking the breach was empty, before repeating the process to double-check. He lowered the hammer and reset the safety catch. Jessica stepped forward, looking up again into his eyes and opening her mouth.

Cavus slipped the muzzle into her mouth, resting the barrel along her tongue. Slowly, gently, he eased the barrel further into her mouth until her throat muscles tightened – she squeezed her eyes shut and swallowed away the gagging sensation. After a brief pause, he eased it back further – until she gagged again. She tried to speak and her eyes opened wide as she struggled to take a breath. Cavus held the back of her neck to prevent her from pulling away. He held her retching for a moment before releasing her. As she gasped for air, he moved in for a deep and passionate kiss. She reciprocated, gasping for air between forcing her tongue into his mouth. She bit his lip and the blood mixed with the oil and metal taste in her mouth.

Moaning in time with Cavus kissing, she allowed him to push her on to the bed. Bringing her own hands above her head and gripping the bed rails, he snapped the second shackle on to her free wrist.

'Cavus, we need a safe word. I'm nervous, I hardly know you.'

'No safe word, Jess. I will do what I think you want me to do. If I get it wrong, you will tell me to stop. Ok?'

The morning sun penetrated the shack windows as the temperature rose, Jessica realising she should have closed the shutters and turned on the fan. A bead of sweat ran into her eye and she blinked with the stinging, unable to wipe it away.

'Ok. Go on.'

Cavus pushed the bikini top over her chest. Jessica watched as he moved to her shorts and pulled them down and off. He laid the gun across her belly and gently kissed her mouth.

'Take off your shirt, Cavus.'

He smiled but ignored the request. Keeping the pistol flat, Cavus slid it across her belly, over her chest and back over her belly. Lifting it by the handle, he carefully dragged it along her outer thigh – the sight lightly scratching her skin. He stopped at the top of her leg and laid it flat again. Without speaking, he studied her face.

Jessica stared back. She felt the heat from his chest against her torso. Sweat ran down her sides, collecting where her back touched the bed throw. Cavus raised his eyebrows, questioning. Jessica licked her dry lips again; she trembled a little and felt slightly ridiculous. She nodded.

'Yes, Jess? Yes, what?'

Her voice barely audible, she cleared her throat.

'Yes, Cavus. Do it.'

She moved her legs apart, holding his gaze as she felt the cold steel of the pistol barrel move inside her legs. As the muzzle of the pistol pushed against her, she felt herself involuntarily push down on to it. She heard herself moan.

Jessica woke, beads of sweat covering her body – naked, except for the bikini top pushed off her breasts. Cavus had re-holstered the gun and removed the handcuffs. He sat in bed, looking cool in the oven of a room. Jessica purred, stretching, and smiled up at him.

'Cavus, what must you think? I can't believe we just did that shit, on a first date!'

He tinkled his boyish giggle and tousled her damp hair.

'You are on holiday. You can let down your hair.'

Jessica switched on the fan and opened the door, allowing more air to circulate; the voile curtain shimmered in the sea breeze.

'And then I fell asleep; some hostess.'

She drank a tumbler of water from the tap, bringing two glasses back to bed. Holding the water in both hands, she sat astride Cavus and kissed him fully on the mouth – slipping her now cool tongue into his mouth. Setting down the glasses, she pulled his shirt over his head.

'So, soldier, where were we?' She gasped. 'The tattoo. A dagger!'

'It is nothing to worry about Jess. It is a regiment thing. We may not have them anymore because of our covert work, but most guys of my age and older already have them. Jess?'

'Sorry, Cavus. It made me go cold. I have seen one before, cut in half by a… a real bullet.'

Cavus chuckled.

'You like to date your soldiers, Jess.'

Jessica smiled and nodded; trying to blink away the memory and excitement at seeing the healed bullet wounds, which she had touched and kissed on Albay's chest, back and hip. She realised how any soldier, this soldier, might be shot and perhaps not survive. She remembered the list of the fallen that Kenan had given her to read in Gallipoli. For a moment, she nuzzled into Cavus's warm hair, smelling the shampoo and lemon cologne, before springing back onto her knees smiling, straddling him again.

They made love. Sometimes Jessica dropped her body so that her nose and forehead touched his. Sometimes she straightened or arched her back, clutching at her own hair with both hands or gripping his hands, interlocking fingers. Throughout the entire time, they maintained eye contact.

It was Cavus' turn to fall asleep. Jessica lay bathed in swcat; hc had only a few beads on his forehead and none on his body. Jessica traced the tattoo with her finger and then the tip of her tongue. She remembered doing the same to Albay just a few weeks earlier – but in a beautiful boutique hotel and not a hot beach shack with a tin roof. She ran the tip of her tongue down his body and over his firm, muscular belly.

She continued lower. Sleepily he placed his hand on the back of her head, gripping a handful of hair. It was obvious to Jessica that he was too spent to continue their lovemaking, so she firmly eased his hand away and flipped onto her back, resting her head on his hips and pulling his hand across her chest.

Sleep would not come in the heat and following her earlier nap, so she gave up trying and moved to the shower, and then outside to the picnic table. On the way, she shuttered the windows against the sun and took cold beers from the gas-fridge.

The couple walked the length of the riverbank and strolled along the jetty, stopping to eat fish and bread at the fisher's cooperative café. The servings were huge, but both ordered more and laughed easily at their private joke – how their lovemaking had left them so hungry.

'Are you busy tomorrow, Cavus? Sightseeing? Or are you at a loose end?'

'If you are available, Jess, I would love to spend a lazy day around Koyaka, maybe take your kayak out? But I understand if…'

'I'd love to Cavus. I think we should drive and hike to the waterfall, have a picnic and, you know, all that. Then drive back for an afternoon here on the beach.'

'I should stay in the village…'

'Are you working?'

'No, no. Nothing like that. It is just, busy, at the moment. However, you are right, I am on holiday. The Republic will have to defend itself for a day. I would love to visit the waterfall with you.'

Jessica shrugged. 'Up to you.'

The conversation fell away, and the couple finished the fish in silence. Both made to speak at the same time.

'Sorry Jess. Go on, you say.'

'No Cavus – you speak. I insist.' Silence returned for a minute before Cavus continued.

'I was just going to say Jess. I will go back to work in less than two weeks.'

Jessica returned his coy look with a blank stare of her own.

'Right.'

'So I am saying that we will not see so much of each other once I go back. I travel around the country and…'

'Cavus. Sweetheart. I invited you in for a coffee as you walked past. Don't be so arrogant, I haven't fallen in love with you; get over yourself.'

Jessica did not intend to sound so harsh and was pleased to see a look of relief on his face, rather than offense. He was obviously a man used to breaking hearts.

As they rose to continue their stroll, she slipped her hand under his arm to reset their first date together.

Following a day walking through the forest, along to the neighbouring beach and back again, he walked her to the shack, and they kissed goodnight.

The following day they drove the short distance and walked into the hills to swim at the waterfall. Pools formed at the base of the falls, each one warmer the further away from the waterfall. The waterfall itself was cold and refreshing in the heat of the summer day.

They swam in only shorts. Jessica floated on her back, the force of the falls easing her around the edges of the larger pool. She watched Cavus climb the slippery rocks. Every few steps he stopped to assess the height and check that Jessica was watching. She smiled to herself, *boys will be boys.*

She watched him move away from the falls towards a high ledge, from where she assumed he would dive. At least twenty feet above the water and with the depth of the pool unknown, she felt her stomach tighten at the thought of him jumping. It seemed a silly risk to take, but equally she wanted him to take that risk to impress her. She swam further away to watch the dive.

Loose shale skidded from under his foot at the same time his hand slipped on a slimy hold. He fell away bent double, as he used his core strength in an attempt to recover the dive and to manoeuvre himself further from the cliff. Jessica felt her stomach flip as he fell. She screamed as he back-flopped into the water; Jessica powered towards the impact spot.

The waterfall turned the otherwise clear water into a thrash of bubbles and air. With zero visibility she dived under the mayhem; eyes wide open in the cold water. The waterfall pulled her up and away from the spot where Cavus had entered the pool. Jessica dived again, forcing herself deeper. She saw nothing of Cavus. Gasping a breath of air and spray, Jessica turned to dive again but felt a hand around her ankle, pulling her under the surface. Two hands worked up her leg, waist and torso. With her ears crackling from the depth and the force of the falls directly above her, she hovered with neutral buoyancy and came face-to-face with a grinning Cavus. He pulled her towards him; she wrapped her legs around his waist and they kissed. As they held each other close, Jessica realised she could cry underwater; tears of relief. She also realised she trusted this stranger enough to allow him to hold her away from oxygen. As her lungs stung, the couple bobbed to the surface at the edge of the cascading falls.

They swam to the edge of the pool and helped each other onto the bank. Cavus made to draw her close again, but she pushed back against his chest. Once she had the room, Jessica swung at Cavus, catching his jaw with a slap of her open hand.

'You idiot!'

'Yes, I am fine, thank you for asking.'

Jessica took another swing at Cavus, tears streaming down her face. Despite the accuracy and speed of the punch, Cavus caught it easily with an open palm.

'I thought you were dead! I thought you had broken your back!'

'Sorry, but when I saw you half-naked, diving to find me, I was in no hurry for the rescue to be over.'

Cavus squeezed her clenched fist in the palm of his hand and twisted back her wrist, forcing her to comply. Jessica relaxed her shoulders, looking directly at him. At the crucial moment, she opened her mouth to accept his, tilting her head slightly, before delivering a head-butt directly to the bridge of his nose.

His head snapped backward, and he fell into the pool, holding his nose in one hand and laughing.

'You ever push yourself on me again and I will cut off your bollocks!'

Jessica grabbed at the pile of clothes and stomped away towards the car. By the time Cavus had collected the remaining belongings and trotted after Jessica, she had already driven the car to the edge of the track. As Cavus neared, she drove down the track. He managed to run alongside until they reached the dry bed of a stream, taking the opportunity to jump into the passenger seat.

Jessica drove onto the metalled road towards home. She spoke first.

'Sorry if I broke your nose.'

'Nothing broken Jess, just my pride. Special Forces Training never prepared me for Jessica Khan!'

Jessica glared at her passenger.

'How do you know my name?'

'You told me. Or I saw it in your house. I saw your house Tapu on the side.'

Jessica continued to glare at Cavus as he became uncomfortable with her driving.

'Jess, please look where you are going.'

'Nobody scares me and nobody forces me to do anything that I don't want to. Understood?'

'I just thought that, after yesterday…'

'Well you *thought* wrong!'

'Ok. Sorry I fell and I am sorry you attacked me. It won't happen again, promise.'

The couple smiled at each other, but both realised the second and probably last date was now over. Back at the shack, Jessica allowed Cavus to towel-dry her hair and back; but she did not invite him to stay.

'You are a strange girl, Jess. You push things and then act all hurt when they tip out of your control.'

'Ahh, that is so sweet. You said that as if I had asked for your opinion or even care what you think.'

'Ok. You are nothing if not direct. May I ask you something, please?'

'Of course.'

'Something else has upset you. Not just the waterfall today. Ok, I messed around after I fell, but it was not planned. Tell me, what else has happened, please?'

Jessica replied, her tone thoughtful rather than combatant.

'Cavus, I don't enjoy being with you. It's simple.'

Cavus showed no outward emotion.

'Why? I am not arguing and to be honest Jess, I do not really care. I have a couple of weeks off, in a seaside village; I will not be lonely for long. I am just confused at how quickly you drank me in, to spit me out again.'

'I don't owe you an explanation, Cavus.'

They sat facing each other across the picnic table, shaded from the high afternoon sun by the eucalyptus trees and cooled by the rushing river, just yards away. Cavus did not respond. He took a long drink of beer from his bottle and Jessica mirrored him with hers.

'Alright, I will tell you. But this is not a conversation, understand? This is not really any of your business; this is about me Cavus, not you.
'You scare me. Your reactions are quicker than mine. You read me better than I read you. Even when I made love to you, really you were making love to me. You know stuff, you know who I am. And you remind me too much of a friend of mine; kissing you is like dancing on my grave and I don't like it; you even look like him. Finally, I am scared that I trust you too much – nobody does what we did with the gun - on a first-date over coffee, for Christ's sake.'

'Jess, you haven't gone and fallen in love with me, by any chance?'

'Fuck off, Cavus. I said this wasn't a conversation.' Jessica broke eye contact.

'Have you ever had stuffed mussels, Jess?'

'What?'

'They are mussels…'

'I know what they are, Cavus! I am just not sure of the relevance to our conversation.'

'So it is a conversation, or it isn't a conversation?'

Jessica felt her blood pressure rise. She wanted to punch him from across the table but knew he would be two steps ahead or that he would decide to absorb the blow without flinching.

'Stuffed mussels Cavus – you were saying.'

'I will see if the fisherman has any good mussels. On the way back I can pick up the white-wine for cooking and I think you are out of chillies, but you have rice, almonds, oil and peppers…'

'See! I did not know I was out of chillies, how do you know?'

'… and I will cook for you. You will not ask me to stay tonight. I will go back to my hotel. Tomorrow I will kite-surf and maybe meet a new friend and you will watch the soldiers walking past again.' The couple smiled at each other. 'And we will stay just friends.'

'I don't believe this Cavus. Ok, whatever.'

CHAPTER 11 – LIVE A LITTLE

While Cavus shopped, Jessica showered and changed. First into her expensive silk dress and then again into a grey cotton slip-dress, she had purchased in the village. Jessica normally felt comfortable in short-dresses, but today she pulled on thigh-length fitted white shorts to avoid any misunderstandings.

As Cavus cooked and stuffed the muscles, Jessica tossed salad and sliced a large flat loaf of village bread.

Without asking, Cavus brought the old radiogram from the corner of the room where Jessica had it set as a display shelf – showing framed A4 prints of her friend Amara, her ex-boyfriend Chris, her two nieces and her soon to be Goddaughter April, which she recently downloaded from Facebook.

'I'm not sure it actually works, Cavus. But... oh, ok just try it then, why don't you?'

The radiogram came to life playing Turkish folk music. Jessica was pleased with how quickly she was picking up the language, but to the best of her knowledge, the song was about a boy liking a girl's aubergines. A glass of merlot down, she giggled.

'The last time this radio played was when Noah's Ark grounded – yet it plays modern music! How clever.'

Cavus smiled at her joke. 'Well, Noah did land in Turkey, so you might be right.'

Jessica snorted.

'Come on, you are joking,'

'No, He chose to land at mount Ararat. Maybe a day east of here, you must visit. He chose well, it is beautiful.' Jessica felt more relaxed than earlier and she allowed herself to grip his hand.

'The last person to tell me stories like this…' She let the words fade. 'Anyway, where he landed was random, he had no influence.'

'You misunderstand. I meant He chose to land Noah in Turkey, Him – God.'

'Turkey Turkey Turkey.'

'Yes, it is a wonderful place.'

Before the banter could continue, an urgent-sounding announcement interrupted the music. Cavus held up his hand for silence, at the same time looking at his phone before powering down.

'There is a coup. Jets are fighting over Istanbul. The Air Force is leading a revolt against the President's government.' Cavus spoke evenly and without surprise.

He left the shack and trotted toward his Bed-and-Breakfast, returning wearing his bomber jacket and the service pistol holstered onto his belt. He carried a sports bag.

'Jess, I need your phone, please.'

Jessica handed him her phone and without asking for the password, he swiped on to the home screen and opened a WhatsApp icon, which had not worked for Jessica since leaving the U.K. Using both thumbs he tapped messages, glancing at the returns before responding again. For the first time, Jessica noticed sweat run on his face and neck.

She saw Elvis jump to his feet on the small veranda, at the same time as Cavus's head snapped to attention. He placed his finger to his lips and gestured for Jessica to leave the shack. Outside stood two Jandarma. The female officer spoke.

'Cavus Salepci here, please?'

For no good reason that sprung to mind, Jessica lied.

'Cavus? No. Not now. He was here earlier.' Jessica saw the police van parked outside the Bed-and-Breakfast. 'I think he is staying in that hotel. Maybe you can find him there.'

The female lightly held Jessica's wrist as the male officer brushed past and into the shack, his hand resting on his holstered pistol. Jessica heard the bathroom door open and close. The soldier returned and spoke to his colleague.

'He said you have food and wine glasses for two.'

'Yes. I hope Cavus will drop by. We argued today and I think he is avoiding me. You know, men just can't take a joke sometimes; I head-butted him.' The female stared at Jessica without blinking. Jessica held her gaze. She handed Jessica a business card.

'If he comes here, you call this number. Understand? And tell him to report to Koyaka barracks immediately.'

'Hang on love, you can't give me orders, What has he done wrong?'

'Yes, love, I can give you orders. If he reports to barracks, then he has done nothing wrong and neither of you will go to prison. Understand, love?'

'Are you…'

'Yes, I am threatening you. You will sit in prison for weeks, even if we decide not to charge you with harbouring a fugitive. Best not play games with me, love.'

Jessica's face burned, she felt exposed and vulnerable. Two fighter jets screamed above them towards the hills and the direction of neighbouring Marmaris. Jessica automatically ducked, the soldiers stood without flinching.

'Yes. If I see him, I will tell him.' The soldier continued to stare. 'And tell you.'

The two Jandarma strolled around the shack and back to their van. Jessica returned to inside the shack; certain the soldiers could hear her heart pounding from across the street.

Cavus sat on the bed. The cover and mattress dislodged.

'What? You hid at the back of the mattress?'

Cavus managed a weak smile, his face pale with apprehension.

'They do not think I am stupid enough to be here. But they will be watching.'

'What have you done, Cavus? And no bullshit! You did not say your name is Salepci. You are related to Albay. I knew I recognised you.'

'I have done nothing wrong. Some of my regiment is involved in the coup. We have been ordered to return to barracks.'

'So, return to barracks, then.'

'Thank you for the advice. But my superiors will decide where my duty lays – not a girl from another continent.'

'Ok, so do it elsewhere, not in my house.'

'I don't think you realise just how involved you already are, *disi aslant.*'

'Why did you call me lioness, Cavus? What is going on?'

Cavus met her stare.

'There will be a new temporary government tomorrow. Until then, you must do as I tell you.' He checked his watch, walking to the radiogram. Still switched on, the station was off air. 'Screwdriver please, Jess.'

Jessica did not move. With a sigh, he brushed past and rummaged in the cupboard under the sink.

'Top drawer, left.'

Cavus retrieved the screwdriver and dismantled the radiogram, unscrewing the top and lifting it to the floor. Jessica stared at equipment packed into the cavity. She said nothing; Cavus was not in a communicative mood. Checking his watch again, he removed components of what appeared to be a flat-pack toy glider. The middle section held electronics. The nose section, wings and tail assembled from piece parts. Completed, it measured around four feet in length. Cavus then removed a light metallic cylinder, screwing down the cap using the same screwdriver, until it snapped to a stop. His hands trembled a little and sweat formed on his face and neck.

'Can I ask…'

'Christ Jess! Shut-up, let me concentrate.'

He fitted the cylinder under the middle section, sat back onto the floor and gasped, almost hyperventilating. Calming his breathing, Cavus pushed his sweaty hands over his face and through his hair. He removed a slim square control panel from the radiogram and what Jessica assumed to be a shortwave radio and handset of similar dimensions – both items looking like car radio sets. Again, he checked his watch. He replaced the top cover and told Jessica to scroll for a news station. Cavus swiped open Jessica's phone and checked the WhatsApp icon, seeing nothing he powered it down.

Voices blared from the radio and the couple jumped, looking at each other with a smile. Cavus took his small personal protection pistol and spare magazines from his bag and slipped them into the bomber jacket, zipping closed the pockets. Blue and red lights lit the outside garden as they listened to a van drive past, slowly.

'Cavus – don't shout at me. Which side, of what, are we on, here?'

'We Jess, are on the side of the Turkish Republic.'

'Prick! Is that the best you can manage?'

'Ok. First, I want you to tell me something and don't lie. You need to start trusting me, for your own safety.'

'*Start* trusting you. You're not the one who had a pistol pointed up her… at her, you know what I am saying! And I let you hold me under the water until you decided to let me breathe. You are the one who needs to open up, pal.'

'Why did you go to Tehran and then stop in Eshtehard?'

'I didn't! I have never even heard of Eshtehard.'

'The Revolutionary Guard has a base. And you do like a uniform.'

'Is that supposed to be funny? I have been no further east than Cappadocia.'

Cavus studies her face. He clearly believed her answer.

'Ok Jess. You need to understand something. The Turkish Army is a third of the Republic. We have the courts and Constitutional Court, we have the civil government with our elected president, and we have the army. Ok?'

'Yes Cavus, I can count to three.'

'Our president is too big-for-his-boots, as you would say. His ex-friend, Gulen, has infiltrated various institutions and academia, and the president has assumed too much power for himself and his family. Between them, they influence the courts, which are no longer independent. The army has a duty to the Republic, the constitution and the people, to protect our secular democracy. We have no choice. We have to act. We are not criminals. The military will govern until the people elect new leaders.'

'And what if they re-elect the same president? Didn't you throw him out of office once before?'

'It is unlikely he will be re-elected.'

'You can't say that for sure.' Cavus shrugged. 'So this is a free democracy, so long as the people vote for whom you tell them. And while this charade unfolds, you make model aeroplanes and I get threatened by a dyke with a gun!'

Cavus checked his watch again, as the short-wave radio removed from inside the radiogram sounded.

Yurtta Sulh Konsey. Aslan Uyur, simdi.

Jessica understood the end of the message to say 'lion sleeps, now'. Cavus spoke into the handpiece, a single word of acknowledgment.

'Evet.'

Switching off the news on the radiogram, he collected the aeroplane from the floor, attaching a line with a toggle to the tail. Checking outside the shack, he laid the aeroplane in one corner of the garden and the control box at the opposite corner, near the river. Making adjustments to the control box, the aeroplane purred awake – propellers spinning at the nose and wings.

Trotting back, Cavus collected the plane. Holding it above his head he jogged to the control box, releasing the plane with an extra flick from the line-woomera. The toggle released the line and the drone glided over the river, dipping slightly before the automatic controls kicked in and adjusted the flight path, for the drone to climb over the reeds and into the dark sky.

'Cavus. Who is the lion and what are you doing?'

'I am saving the lives of Turkish soldiers and civilians, Jess. I am doing the honourable work of a soldier.'

'You are killing someone! God Cavus, you must stop this.'

'Turkish soldiers are fighting with Turkish crowds and with other Turkish soldiers. This one act will end the madness.'

Jessica felt an unwelcome wave of excitement, sending tingles and goosebumps across her flesh. She also felt bile rise in her throat. If this act was for the good of everyone, win-win, then maybe she wanted to be part of it. The thought disgusted her, but she could not push it from her mind. Cavus hunched over the tiny green glow of the control screen, making minor adjustments to two dials - not operating the joystick, but allowing the autopilot to direct the drone.

'Cavus? Can I see?'

Cavus held the control box to allow Jessica to see the tops of fir trees and the occasional lights from houses whip past. She took the box and cradled it in her lap.

'Will we see him Cavus?' She spoke in little more than a whisper. 'Will we see him…'

'The drone is carrying high explosive, we will see nothing on impact, but yes, we will see a moment before. You must look away; the sight will never leave your dreams.'

Jessica studied the small screen again. She held the joystick. An unintentional smile crossed her lips and her breathing laboured. She bit hard into her lower lip.

'His name?'

'Recep Tayyip Erdogan.'

'President?'

'He is on holiday in Marmaris. The coup is timed for when he is out of Istanbul. I need to take this now.'

Cavus reached for the control box. Jessica let him take it but kept her hand on the joystick. The screen glowed into images of Marmaris - hotels, houses, streetlights and car lights. Cavus eased a slide on the control box and took control, operating the joystick with Jessica's hand still gripping it. Using small nudging adjustments, Jessica felt Cavus circle the drone around a huge private house. She saw two SUVs parked close to an outbuilding on the edge of a large swimming pool. She saw six figures stood around an open car door. One figure stood apart from the others in the centre of their circle. Jessica guessed the lone figure was using a phone. He now climbed into the car.

'There! It is him, Cavus. There!'

Cavus turned a dial to zoom the camera. The figure had a slight green hue, but Jessica recognised the thinning scalp. The angle of the drone captured the strong nose and permanent smile of the president. Cavus eased the joystick forward as the president, then the car, then the concrete drive, swirled to fill the screen.

The image died. The screen now a blank green glow. At that moment, the sky towards Marmaris flashed as with sheet lightning. Seconds later,

Jessica jumped and squealed at the sound of a dull thud.

'Shit Cavus. We did it.' Jessica jumped onto her knees. She grabbed his face. 'What have we done?'

She kissed him hard on the mouth before pulling back and vomiting. She moved to kiss Cavus again, but he placed a calming hand on her chest.

'Jess, we need to move. I will leave you soon and you need to keep a low profile. Things will be odd for a few days. You tell nobody about this – ever. I will contact you soon. Maybe one week.'

'Do you need a lift?'

Cavus laughed.

'I don't think it works that way. You must not go outside the village. I will go for a brief camping trip and my people will whisk me back to Istanbul soon, *Insallah*. Jess, you have enough adrenalin pumping around you to supply a hospital for a month. Listen to me, it won't last. You won't sleep, you won't eat, you mustn't drink too much alcohol. You will feel sick and depressed. This is a big night for you and you will never be the same again. Now, I must go.'

Cavus threw the control box into the river and returned to the shack. Jessica followed to find him reassembling the old radiogram. Packing the small radio into his bag, he slipped on his bomber jacket and kissed Jessica on the forehead. They did not speak.

He opened the door as two gunshots rung-out. One bullet blistered the back wall of the living room and another thudded into the open door. Cavus fell backward onto the floor. He drew his service pistol and fired three shots wildly into the darkness. Before he could move back inside the shack, hands grabbed his feet as a second body slammed him with a riot shield. The three soldiers grappled in the doorway and Jessica joined the fray, punching and pulling at the soldier holding the shield. Jessica could see other soldiers trying to squeeze into the doorway to subdue Cavus.

Launching herself at the soldier with the shield, she propelled them both over Cavus, landing on top of the second soldier. Hands grabbed Jessica's hair and throat from her left as Cavus rolled to her right, firing more shots towards his assailants.

Elvis took this opportunity to free his new mistress from the arresting soldier. He locked jaws around the soldier's upper arm and, flipping onto his back, used his weight to drag the soldier to the ground. Screaming, the soldier reached for his pistol as Jessica kicked away his hand. The soldier with the shield now drew his pistol and fired at Elvis. The gun was less than one foot from Jessica's ear, but she still heard the screech from Elvis as the huge dog rolled over and whimpered, before letting out a second shriek and blindly snapping at Jessica's assailant, fighting to protect her with his dying breath.

Elvis fell silent. Jessica heard only muffled noises above the ringing in her ears. More shots fired and three soldiers peeled off, chasing Cavus towards the river. Jessica was dragged to her knees and handcuffed. She fell forward, her head resting against the thick fleece of Elvis. She could barely hear her own wailing. She sobbed for Cavus, for the six men she had helped kill, for herself and for her pathetic dog, who died trying to fight the Turkish Army to protect her. The female Jandarma soldier, who had visited earlier, walked back from the river's edge, shouting orders to search for Cavus. He had jumped into the river – crossing into the reeds or swimming downstream in the darkness. The soldier stopped at Jessica, her face still buried in Elvis's coat, and kicked her hard in the upper stomach. Jessica replaced her wailing with rasping gasps for breath.

Jessica now sat on a plastic garden chair. Her landlord's van pulled to the side of the road. Ignoring a raised hand from the female Jandarma soldier, Oglan bolted from the passenger door to Elvis. His father, with both hands raised, walked slowly towards his son whilst explaining to the Jandarma that the dog was theirs. Jessica struggled to stand handcuffed, and walked to the boy.

'Oglan. I am sorry. He was so brave.'

The boy turned to face Jessica, tears streaming down his cheeks. He sniffed and spat in Jessica's face. Oglan's father grabbed the boy's shoulders, leading him to the van and returning with a blanket to wrap and carry away Elvis. The second remaining soldier helped carry the dog to the van.

The female soldier searched the shack but brought out nothing Jessica could see, other than Jessica's passport, journal and her house-rental document. Jessica had lost track of her phone; it may be with Cavus. She remained quiet, sat on the plastic chair, wondering why she had not yet been taken away.

'Um... excuse me, Miss. Is it possible to talk with my Embassy please? Or maybe a lawyer?'

The two soldiers exchanged glances and smiled at each other.

'Shut-up.'

Jessica nodded and bowed her head. She could do with her friend Amara here, right now.

The soldier's radios crackled into life and the female held a conversation, turning away from Jessica. The soldiers searching for Cavus returned to the shack and stood awkwardly as the female glared at them, still talking into her radio. She barked an instruction to the younger male soldier, who then removed Jessica's handcuffs.

'Khan. We have been ordered to return to barracks, your lucky day. You will stay here, right here. You will not even go to the shop. Understood? When we are released from barracks, I shall visit you again. If you abscond, I will find you and you risk being shot for... oh, I don't know, but I will think of something. And finally, if Salepci turns up, you call me. Understood?'

'Yes. But I don't have a phone...'

'Shut-up!'

Jessica nodded. The soldiers left.

Jessica waved a reassuring hand towards the Bed and Breakfast owner, who glared back and slammed closed her shutters.

Bruised and tired, Jessica lay on her bed and closed her eyes to the image of the six men, whom she had done nothing to help. Six men with families, lovers, parents and friends. Worse – she had felt a rush of excitement as they were extinguished like the images in some perverse X-Box game. She imagined some of the men had looked up at the drone with expressions of desperation and fear. Others looked happy and carefree. Sleep did not come.

CHAPTER 12 – PRIORITISE MYSELF

Jessica managed to drink water but felt nauseous and unable to eat. She lay or sat on the bed, or paced the shack. She had no friends in the village, no phone, no passport and no way of leaving or calling for help. For the first time in her life, she wished she had died during the fight – to ease the pain in her conscience.

Hearing a noise outside, she crept to the door and peering through the small window saw Cavus dragging the kayak to the river. She slipped out and padded barefoot across the garden.

'Cavus…'

Cavus spun around, his hand moving to the handle of his service pistol.

'Christ Jess! Are you trying to finish me off?'

'Cavus, why did they not arrest me? What do we do, now?'

'You must stay brave. All Jandarma are ordered back to barracks for the moment. Only the civil police are on the streets. There have been problems. You had best come with me.'

'Where too? They threatened to kill me if I go anywhere.'

'I am meeting a helicopter and going to Greece. You had best come with me. Otherwise, once they arrest you, they will make you explain what happened – that will not be good for me, my family, the Republic, or for you. In the kayak please, right now.'

Jessica sat in the front, still wearing her thin cotton dress, shorts and no shoes. Cavus stepped into the rear and pushed off into the current of the river. Ordering Jessica to lie flat, Cavus used the paddle as a rudder, steering the kayak close to the reeds as the flow took them into the bay. Paddling past the jetty they came close to a police launch and several small fishing boats, the occupants talking about the coup over pots of tea and fried fish. An Anatolian Shepherd dog, smaller than Elvis, walked along the jetty keeping pace with the kayak, until they left it behind at the jetty end, tail wagging slowly.

The bay is wide at Koyaka and narrows slightly towards the open Aegean. Bodrum sits at the end of the right finger of land, with Marmais over the hill of the left finger. All boats had been ordered into port and the bay was silent, except for the occasional fighter jets screaming overhead and making a loop towards the Greek Islands of Kos and Rhodes, before flying over Marmaris and back towards Koyaka.

They paddled away from the village and into blackness for two hours before Cavus started the tiny two-stroke engine; continuing to paddle to steer and increase speed. The budding Buck Moon illuminated the cliffs enough for them to loom larger and more menacing. Jessica tried to imagine they were in the Slovenian caves and that Cavus was her confident, safe and reassuring guide. She asked about his plan and his relationship with Albay. Like picking at a scab, she could not help but ask for the explanation she was dreading – that she had slept with father and son. This minor act of self-harm, diverting her from the agony of her bigger troubles and her troubled conscience. Cavus said nothing, other than the occasionally whispered *shut-up*.

Jessica's arms ached. Her upper body soaked in sweat and her legs wet and cold from the sea spray. Her lungs burned with exertion. Occasionally she stopped paddling to rest, before Cavus would prompt her to continue with the sole of his foot. On one occasion, she dropped her head onto the paddle and fell asleep. Cavus allowed her to rest for ten minutes before spray woke her and she resumed paddling.

Hearing a helicopter, long before Jessica, Cavus pulled the kayak under a rock overhang on the left cliff, to avoid the thermal cameras. They rested for twenty minutes and drank a little bottled water until the aircraft had completed its sweep and moved to the other side of the Bodrum peninsula. The motor ran-out of petrol; Cavus removed and dropped it into the water to reduce weight, before continuing the journey towards the open sea.

Jessica lost track of time but guessed it was around three o'clock in the morning before they reached the tip of the Datca peninsula to the left. The glow of Bodrum's lights now visible to her right side. Straight ahead, lay the lights of the Greek Island Kos and further left she saw the glow of lights from Rhodes. The open sea swell was significantly greater than within the bay and she felt, for the first time, that it could overwhelm the kayak; they had no lifejackets.

Cavus headed for a spit of rock jutting from the Datca peninsula and beached the kayak in a pebble cove, barely larger than the boat. There had once been a, now dry, stream or waterfall that created a slightly reduced incline to the rock face, but which was still too steep for Jessica to attempt without ropes.

'Cavus, I can't go on; I have no strength.'

Cavus stretched and jogged on the spot, working his muscles and improving circulation.

'Ok *disi aslan…*'

'Please, Cavus. Do not call me that. You know my name.'

'Jess. We will climb as high as you can, then I will push you up further. Then I will drag you higher. Then we will be safe at the top. We will be lifted to Greece by helicopter and get you back to the U.K. Believe me, *Kizim…*'

'Jessica!'

'… the alternative, is not an option.'

Jessica began the climb; resting for a moment to catch her breath and realising she had managed less than Cavus's height, who still stood on the beach. She felt tears sting her eyes before laughing and slipping painfully back to the ground, Cavus's taking her weight and helping her stand. Jessica hung her arms loosely around his neck.

'We need a Plan B, my love. Otherwise, I will end up dead at the bottom of this cliff.'

'That is a risk I must take.' Jessica stared, wide-eyed. 'The helicopter cannot reach us here. We have no choice; plan A. You can do it.'

'Oh well. If you are prepared to risk me dying, I suppose I had better get a move on.'

Cavus added the half bottle of water to his bag, slung the straps over his shoulders like a rucksack, and helped Jessica scramble up the cliff until she was out of his reach. He climbed effortlessly behind her, dragging and pushing Jessica as she hauled herself higher. The cliff angle improved slightly as they followed the dried rivulet, allowing the couple to make some progress.

Stopping where the cliff became vertical again, Jessica looked down and realised without emergency services to hand, they were now at the point where Cavus felt prepared to risk her life.

'This is not so bad, Jess. The footholds are good. Don't look down. Maintain three points of contact. Don't fall off.'

Cavus smiled at his last remark and unexpectedly received one back. Jessica had indoor climbed with a boy she dated from college, the two had caved, and abseiled in Cheddar – but with ropes. She took a moment to plan her route in the limited light, avoiding an overhang, and commenced the climb. Cavus stayed close behind; however, there was little he could do to assist or keep her safe. Although Jessica had avoided one overhang, she climbed to a second unseen arête.

'We need to go back. I can't do this overhanging arête.'

'You are doing well, Jess. You have chosen the best route. Take the overhang at the diagonal, keep moving to your right.'

Jessica took a few more steps, her back now angled away from the cliff; she felt gravity tugging at her bottom, pulling the weight off her footholds. Her foot bled as she squeezed it against the jagged rock to gain traction. Stretching her right leg to find a small ledge, she gently shifted her weight to realign her body as her left foot slipped from its hold. She let out a weak grunt as her body swung perpendicular, hanging from only her hands.

'I only have a pinch on my left hand. All of my weight is on my right hand. I can't move.'

Cavus stretched his right leg under her left foot, his right foot now supported by only friction against the cliff's surface.

'Jess, I only have a smear. Tail your right leg, bring your left foot onto my shin. Don't put your weight down, I can't support you.'

Jessica adjusted the position of her hanging right foot until her left leg swung in and her toes located against the inside of his calf.

'Calvus, I can do this. I am going to push your leg away. Brace yourself.'

Jessica brought her cheek against the cliff, trying to find any point of support or traction. She pushed her foot against Cavus's leg, which held for just a moment. Jessica's left hand came away, and she swung on just her right hand until her right foot found the ledge, her left foot found a toehold and the heel of her left hand jolted hard against a crimp of rock. Pushing with her left leg and left hand, she relocated her right hand against a jug hold, hauling herself over the arête and standing upright in a narrow chimney of rock.

Cavus took the same route easily with his additional height and stopped, resting against Jessica.

Jessica wore a huge grin, her eyes wide, her voice high and rapid.

'So, that went well. Race you to the top.'

Fitting easily inside the chimney rock formation, Jessica shimmied using her leg muscles to propel herself upwards, clamping herself against the wall of the chimney, before propelling herself again. Cavus only just fitted the chimney and followed more slowly. Jessica waited at the ridge, panting for breath and holding her bleeding foot.

Cavus collapsed next to her, his back against a gentle incline of loose shale. Shaking uncontrollably with adrenalin and the sudden relaxing of her fatigued muscles, Jessica rolled onto Cavus, roughly clutching his face and forcing her mouth against his. Cavus felt the shale move under their weight and flayed his arms, searching for purchase. Jessica screamed and rolled onto her back, laughing.

'*Tanrim* Jessica! You are crazy. Calm down!'

'I did it Cavus. I fucking did it.'

Jessica flipped onto her knees and scampered up the river of loose shale, her light frame skimming the surface. With an extra 30kg of body mass and wearing his kitbag, Cavus followed more cautiously on his hands and knees, digging his boots into the loose shale and keeping his hands flat for traction. At the top stood Jessica, triumphantly.

'Keep down, Jess! This isn't a walk in the park.'

Their new vantage point comprised a small empty plateau of bare rock. They could clearly see Bodrum, Kos and Rhodes. Further away was the glow of Marmaris, and on the opposite side of their peninsula were the distant lights of Datca and Mesudiye.

'Oh Cavus. I left the tea bags in the kayak. Be a love and pop back for them.'

Cavus took the shortwave radio from his backpack. Ignoring Jessica, he spoke a brief message before lying down again onto his back.

'Jess. Come here, lie down.'

'Is that all you think about lover-boy?'

Cavus tried but failed to look stern.

'Seriously love, they are still looking for us. We are in survival mode here.'

As if to reinforce his instructions, the two fighter jets screamed past the couple, flying over the middle of the bay and seemingly at the same altitude as their own position. As they peeled to the left, Jessica felt the sonic boom reverberate through her chest with a deafening thud. The engine heat blasting against her body.

'If you keep down, they won't see us. But this is not good for our helicopter recovery. Hopefully, they will find somewhere more interesting to fly soon. I think their primary job is to look out for "rebel" army helicopters, let the Greeks know Turkey is still secure, and remind the population exactly who has the big toys. This could not be worse for our helicopter trip.'

The couple lay back and stared at the impressive show of stars, the milky way clear above the light from the almost full moon. The radio burst into life, making Jessica start as Cavus reached for the volume. Over the crackle of the radio, Jessica recognised Albay's voice. Cavus refitted the earpiece and whispered into the handset. He moved away from Jessica as the conversation became agitated, urgent.

'*Kahretsin!*' Jessica seldom heard Cavus swear. He took a monocular from the bag and searched the narrow strait separating them from Kos.

'What did Albay say, Cavus? Talk to me, calm down man, you are hyper. Calm down.'

Cavus pushed her away, walking a few yards in an erratic zigzag, before retracing his steps and grabbing Jessica by the shoulders. He opened his mouth to speak, but no words came out. Thrusting Jessica away again, she stumbled and fell. Before she could complain, he stepped forward, gathered her into his arms and hugged her close to his chest.

'Sorry, Jess. Sorry.'

'Cavus enough! No harm done. What is going on?'

'No Jess, I am sorry.'

He broke away again, retracing his manic zigzag. Jessica brought the monocular to her eye to understand for what Cavus was searching. Seeing the lights of Kos flicker into the eyepiece caused a flashback to the drone screen; dropping the monocular onto the bag and stepping back, she gasped.

'Cavus, just tell me what is going on, please? Just say it.'

'They are sending a small boat.'

'Shit! Do we have to climb down again? Christ Cavus!'

'They will climb up with ropes to assist. We will wait here.'

'So why are you so upset? Nothing scares you.'

'You don't understand.'

The noise of pebbles crunching at the base of the cliff distracted Jessica.

'They are here, Jess.'

Cavus walked away from the direction of the noise and Jessica, towards where they had climbed onto the plateau. He sat on his haunches, looking down the length of the shale flow and out over the cliff and into the bay.

Jessica sat next to him, placing her arms around his shoulders, squeezing hard and burying her face into his neck. Cavus sobbed, his shoulders heaving, emitting a low wail. Several minutes passed and without either speaking, his sobs subsided. He stood, wiping his face with the back of his hand. Taking his bomber jacket off and dropping it to the floor, Jessica saw his T-shirt drenched with sweat and tears. He pulled her to her feet. Jessica heard the climber's grappling hooks from the direction of the rescue boat. Cavus held her shoulders, her back to the shale and her bare feet slipping on the loose ground.

'Sorry, Jess. Sorry, I have to. I have been ordered.'

Cavus took a step into the shale, Jessica grabbing his shirt to stop slipping and falling towards the cliff. She screamed.

'No! Cavus no! You don't have to do this, Cavus. Just leave me here and go. Oh God, please Cavus. Don't do this.'

Her feet now had little purchase and she hung from his shirt and from his grip of her shoulders. The more she struggled, the greater chance of falling towards the cliff.

'You don't understand, Jess. We are regrouping and you know too much, you are a danger to us. I am just a soldier.'

He spoke in a low monotone, taking a second step into the shale. Jessica gripped the shirt around his back, hugging tightly into his chest.

'Please no, please.' Her voice now a whisper, gently pleading. 'Please love, no. I love you. Just wait a minute, we can think of something. Darling, I love you. No Cavus, don't do this.'

Cavus slipped slightly in the shale. Stopping, he pushed her shoulders away and towards the cliff. Her strength did not compare with his; feeling as if she was a child in his grip. His hands dug into her shoulders, all feeling squeezed from her arms.

As Jessica tried to steady her feet and make eye contact, she fell, both feet skidding out from behind her. As she slid down his torso, he adjusted his feet, digging his boots into the loose shale for grip. Jessica grabbed at his belt as her weight shifted forward, propelling her head and shoulder between his legs.

Cavus fell forward, landing heavily onto Jessica as she hit the ground on her stomach. Her head snapped forward and her mouth filled with blood. Cavus's groin landed in the small of her back, pushing the air from her lungs – his shins now near her head and his shoulders at her feet. The two slid down the shale towards the cliff, gathering speed. Both grabbed at the loose ground to slow their descent.

With a jolt Jessica's left foot hit solid rock, her extended leg pole-vaulting her onto her back, propelling Cavus further towards the cliff. Still grabbing for a handhold, the couple came to a halt. Blood and dust filled her eyes, mouth and nose.

Cavus now lay half over the cliff, holding on to Jessica's right leg below her knee. He grabbed at her shorts, but already ripped they slid down her legs. They both lay still, frightened to move.

'Cavus. My left leg is wedged. You need to move your grip to my left leg.'

Cavus tried to shift his weight but slipped further, now gripping her ankle. Jessica lay spread-eagled, trying to maximise the surface area in contact with the loose shale. The couple lay still. Jessica felt the faintest of movement, the loose ground shifting steadily beneath her. She imagined she lay in an egg timer, her life slipping away with each second passing. She slowly twisted her head to face Cavus, keeping an even pressure against the ground.

'Cavus, darling. I cannot hold you. I am slipping.'

He released the grip of his right hand and slid it down the ground and over the cliff edge, feeling for anything to grip. Loose grit and dust cascaded over the edge.

'Darling, you must let go. I can't save you, Cavus. You need to let go.'

Cavus slowly brought his right hand back to Jessica's leg, clutching his service pistol and pointing it at Jessica's torso. They made eye contact.

'Cavus, you will not shoot me. You are going to let go and give me a chance to live.'

Jessica smiled weakly, waiting for the flash and bang of the pistol. Wherever it struck her would cause them both to slip and fall.

'Goodbye, my lion. Goodbye. Just let go now. Just let go, my love.'

She gently twisted her right ankle, grinding his hand into the sharp shale. Risking slipping herself, she flexed her leg to dislodge him. She felt laughter rising in her chest; involuntary and inappropriate as she would sometimes feel at funerals or when being chastised as a schoolgirl, or by a lover.

Cavus released the grip of his left hand. For a moment she watched him hover in front of her, suspended in midair, before disappearing silently into the night. His last sight would be of Jessica's repressing her impulsive laughter. The noise of his impact against the moored kayak and beach below would be another memory from this night, which Jessica would take to her grave. The need to laugh left her.

Without Cavus's weight hanging from her leg, Jessica used both hands and her right leg to align her body with her left leg, still wedged against the rock, before crawling up the shale. At the plateau, she saw two black figures crouched to her right – above the cliff leading to the rescue boat. With bare rock beneath her, she rolled silently into a shallow dip and lay on Cavus's discarded bomber jacket. One of the figures stood and scanned the plateau, the moonlight glinting red in the lens of his night-vision goggles.

The second figure held a machine pistol across his chest. Both wore black uniforms with no insignia that Jessica could see in the moonlight. They wore helmets with squat yellow visors, black ballistic vests with high neck protection, oversize knee protectors and high boots. They reminded Jessica of upright armadillos, guest appearances from a Ninja Turtles cartoon.

Jessica rolled one way and back, silently slipping into the oversized black bomber jacket for extra camouflage. She unzipped the pocket and removed the holstered personal protection pistol. Slowly removing the pistol she gently eased back the slide pulling a shell into the breach, carefully sliding it back into position. Releasing the safety catch made a tiny click; both dark figures tensed. She flattened her face against the ground.

The two figures moved apart and crawled towards a point slightly inland of Jessica. She guessed they suspected she was there but had yet to make visual contact. It would not be long before they would have a line of sight.

With each scuffing noise forward that the soldiers made, Jessica wriggled backward and away; her movements in time with theirs, but they were gaining ground. Jessica's right hand extended forward clutching the gun, as her left hand helped propel her backward from the waist. They would soon be at the edge of the dip and she would be visible to them in the moonlight.

Jessica crouched at the beginning of a narrow ledge she hoped would lead on to the main body of the peninsular. There was no obvious path from the soldiers' position, but she realised it would not take them long to catch her if she tried to run away with bare feet. In any event, they would have a clear shot. She raised the pistol.

The first soldier slid into the dip some twenty yards away, lying on his back and reaching for the night-vision goggles. Six feet away from him, the second soldier slipped down, clutching his machine pistol. Jessica was about to lose any slight advantage of surprise.

She aimed the pistol at the centre of the shadowy second soldier, squeezing the trigger three times. The first shot hit the soldier's hand, ricochet off the machine pistol, the second and third slammed into the neck and chest of his bulletproof jacket. Jessica aimed the pistol at the other soldier. He had dropped the goggles and rolled away from his injured colleague. On all fours he scampered back up the incline as Jessica fired three more shots, hitting the back of his knee, between his shoulder blades and in the back of his neck. The last shot slammed the soldier's head and face forward and into the rocky incline.

Jessica dropped the gun and ran along the ledge, leaning inland as the vertical cliff fell away to her left. She crossed a narrow rock bridge and onto the main Datca peninsular, picking up a goat trail. She ran headlong, jumping occasional low gorse bushes that appeared in the moonlight. Her legs ached and her ankles hurt from repeated twists. Her toes and the soles of her feet bled, but she managed to break into a relatively smooth run. Her lungs burned.

The goat trail led on to a dirt track. Except for the occasional stunted Plane Tree and clump of grass or gorse, the landscape remained bare. She slowed to a walk. Her throat dry and swollen; she could no longer swallow. The track merged with a second track and she stopped at a pile of dumped rubbish. Picking out a discarded pair of cotton trousers, Jessica ripped away the legs and tied them around her feet. She took her phone from the pocket of Cavus's jacket and used the torch to search the rubbish; finding and drinking the remains of a water bottle – the top was secure, but the contents green. She watched a catamaran ferry from Marmaris power past and her phone bleeped with a signal notification.

In the seconds of connection, before the ferry drew out of range, Jessica shared her google map location with Belgi. As she tapped an accompanying message to ask for help, she lost the signal.

Shaking with adrenalin and exhaustion, she continued her journey. Passing a farmhouse perched on a narrow terrace growing fruit and vegetables, she collected some under-ripe tomatoes and ate as she walked. The track opened on to a narrow metalled road that had crossed from the opposite side of the peninsula and headed towards Datca.

Against the hill at the side of the road, sat a stone drinking fountain above a livestock trough; rusty-coloured water streamed continuously from the spout. Jessica placed her lips around the spout and drank until her belly filled and her sides cramped into a stitch. This was an exposed location where she could be readily discovered by her assailants, if they were still looking for her, or where she might be arrested by the local Jandarma. She needed to find a phone signal and contact the Embassy, before being discovered.

Jessica sat back against the fountain, water pouring down her neck and back, the bomber jacket now covering her knees. The glow of the morning sun gently illuminated the sky to the east from below the horizon. She leaned forward, resting her head onto her knees to gather the strength to continue. Closing her eyes for a moment, she fell asleep.

The familiar tick-ticking of the Volkswagen Camper engine penetrated her dreams. The sun streamed against the back of her head and waking, she imagined she might be in Gallipoli or Cappadocia. Netter gathered Jessica into her arms and hugged her close.

'My God, Jessica. I thought you are *morte*.'

Jessica opened her eyes and blinked away dust and sunlight. She met Belgi's eyes first.

'Hey, bad penny. How ya doing kid?' Jessica smiled a response.

The couple helped Jessica into the back of the van. She drank two litres of water and ate two bananas in the time it took Belgi to make coffee. Netter gently brushed the tangles and debris from her hair and washed her face in warm water; rubbing vaseline into her cracked lips and antiseptic onto her cuts.

'I said my evil-eye charm would bring you back to me, Netter.'

'Not really, Jess. More like google maps and find-a-phone. The charm was taken off me by a guard outside Tehran.'

'Eshtehard?'

'How did you know? Yes. There was a roadblock, and they had a kind of metal detector thing that bleeped.'

'Shit.' Jessica starred into the middle distance for several seconds. 'It is a tracker. Albay was using it to track me and then his precious bloody box. Shit, shit, shit!'

'You need to start from the beginning, my love.'

'No, I don't. Best you do not know. But how did they track me to Koyaka, when you had the charm?'

Unusually for when Jessica and Netter talked together, Belgi could follow the conversation; Jessica spoke slowly, sounding groggy and fatigued.

'You rented a house in Koyaka. You posted on Facebook, all your *design d'interieur*, how many cushions does one girl need? We knew where you were even before you invited us down. In fact, we were parked outside your house when you sent the google map. We guessed something was wrong – with all the bullet holes, blood, brains and skull everywhere. Time to get the hell out of Dodge City was it, Jessica James?'

'Belgi! Leave her alone.'

'The blood is from my dog. They shot Elvis.'

Jessica picked at grit embedded into the palm of her hand. She had a flashback to the moment Elvis was shot, followed by an uncontrollable flow of images of the body count mounting around her. She gave an involuntary shudder; so violent that Netter and Belgi moved together to hug her.

263

'Well Priscilla, Elvis is back in the building. A big bear, blind, head covered in bandages, wearing a rubber ring around his neck? Has a personal assistant and likes to sit on your veranda? We spoke this morning – to the boy, not the dog. He said he was waiting to speak to you and say sorry. The boy again, I think the dog just wants a bone.'

Jessica looked to Netter for confirmation. Netter nodded. Jessica caught her breath and made a short sobbing sound, but no tears fell.

'Guys, we need to get moving. It isn't safe here. I need to get to the Embassy or Greece. I need to keep out of the way of all sides – Jandarma, rebels, police, authorities. I need…'

'Jessica. Listen to me.' Netter spoke. 'The president has ordered the Jandarma to barracks, but they will be out again later today. The police are all over the roads and towns. Koyaka has some council dustmen dressed in security jackets for the moment, but the police have not moved into the Jandarma controlled villages. The best thing is we drive until we find a phone signal, call the Embassy, get you a lawyer and try to get back to your house, or at least to the village where everyone knows you. Safety in numbers.'

Belgi spoke. 'They can't disappear a little boy, his blind dog, a Belgian man, a Dutch girl and an

English girl all in one day. It would be the worst "walked into a bar" joke ever.'

'Who is acting-president? The president... died.'

'Funny you should say that.' Only Belgi thought it was funny. 'He has the luck of Elvis the dog, as we now say. According to CNN Turk, there was an enormous explosion in the swimming pool of his holiday home, possibly a missile. He and his bodyguard had just climbed into armoured limos, which were tossed across his lawn. It ruined the grass, bits of Mercedes and rubber pink flamingo everywhere. The press is comparing him to Ataturk – he used to trot his horse under fire from the allies at Gallipoli, for a laugh.'

'Pool? He is alive? Are you sure? Did all six survive?'

'Six?'

'I mean the president and his... any other men?'

Netter nodded again; she understood Jessica was never certain when Belgi was messing around.

'Hundreds have died. Soldiers from both sides, civilians, police. Even some poor conscripts who thought they were on a training exercise. A helicopter with nineteen rebels was shot down. But lucky Elvis Erdogan and his cronies are fine.

The cuts and bruises make him look quite the hero. Man of the people.'

'Helicopter?'

Jessica did not look for confirmation. This time the sobs were real and she cried into Netter's neck, barely able to gasp for breath. Belgi laid his hand on the back of her head for a moment before moving to the driver's seat.

'Ya ya ya. She cries when the dog dies, when the dog doesn't die, when the president dies, when the president doesn't die...'

They passed no traffic on the peninsula and very few cars on the main road from Marmaris. Following extensive questioning by the Ankara Embassy over the phone, she was transferred to the Consulate in Izmir where they repeated the process. They advised her to return home to Koyaka, or book into a nearby hotel, or report to the civil police. It was obvious to Jessica that the Embassy and the Consulate were not surprised to hear the part of her story she was prepared to tell them.

They drove through a police roadblock leaving Marmaris, the police waving them through and concentrating more on the cars entering town. They passed two Jandarma posts on the road back to the village. Both had blocks in the road to create a concrete chicane for protection, but the soldiers remained behind the high fences. They drove unhindered into Jessica's garden and parked the van.

Oglan ambled to Jessica, accompanied by Elvis swaying his head from side to side; now blind in both eyes. He sniffed the air between them. Oglan touched Jessica's cut lips with the very tips of his fingers. Elvis lay across her feet.

'Lady. Are you ok?'

'Yeah, Oglan. I'm cool. How's Elvis?'

'Uysal? He is ok. He cannot see now, but he has already seen everything around here, so he does not mind. He will walk between here and my house, but only with me. Here he is ok to walk around your garden. My father asked me to give you this. It is bill for vet. You can pay to vet or me.'

Jessica smiled, taking the invoice. Dropping to her knees she pulled Oglan close for a hug, causing him to lean against Elvis's rump who then thumped his tail in a slow wag. The boy reluctantly allowed Jessica to embrace him for a few moments before squirming away.

'I am too busy, lady. I am going home now.'

Elvis followed the boy as far as the road before returning to the tiny veranda, sniffing the air again for Jessica's scent. Belgi returned from the shack placing bread, cheese and beer onto the picnic table. Jessica dialled Amara.

'Hey Am. You are not going to believe this one.'

Jessica spent the day between her bed, the hammock, and the picnic table. All three took turns to search for a lawyer who would visit and accompany her to the Jandarma. Although one lawyer spent an hour discussing her situation and offering only generic advice, nobody offered to attend.

Jessica cooked pasta with chicken stock cubes for Elvis and pasta in a tomato and chilli sauce for the three humans. She repeated her version of events to Netter and Belgi. Netter made notes. At one point Jessica's voice broke and gripping Netter's wrist, she spoke in a whisper.

'They are going to kill me.'

She was not asking for help, more stating a fact. Blue and red lights illuminated the hotel across the road, the trees and Jessica's shack. The female soldier and her younger sidekick walked to the group of friends.

'*Afiyet olsun.* Take your time, enjoy your food.'

Jessica continued to eat the last of her pasta, forcing down each mouthful against rising bile. Netter and Belgi accompanied her by nibbling at their own meals.

'I have to go. Please inform the Embassy where I am.'

Netter tapped out an email to the Embassy as the soldiers escorted Jessica to the van. Belgi took photographs as they took her away, before following the flashing lights in the campervan. He took more photographs as she was driving into the barracks and one of her being led into the building. They parked the campervan across the road to wait.

Jessica sat in the interview room. The same English looking man, whom she had seen at the border crossing, sat in one corner reading his newspaper. He did not acknowledge her. The female soldier and an officer sat opposite her across a desk, which like the chairs was bolted to the floor.

'I'm saying nothing without a lawyer. I want the Embassy people here.'

The female spoke. 'We don't really do the "no comment" thing here, Jessica.'

'Call me Miss Khan.'

The officer spoke. 'Have you heard of our hat law, Jessica?'

'Hat law? You are joking! Yes, vaguely. It used to be illegal to wear a hat in Turkey or something. Some Ottoman law. Is that why I'm here, because of my hat-wearing?'

'Nearly Jessica. Our founding father Ataturk, at the beginning of our proud republic, passed the Hat Law. We were not an Ottoman, Turkman, an Armenian, Kurd, Georgian, Greek, Franc, with a different fancy hat. We were all Turks, together. The law has never been repealed, it is still illegal to wear a hat in Turkey. You know, we executed a woman for wearing her hat.'

'Oh. How very civilised. Most cosmopolitan.'

'My point is twofold, Jessica. First, we will go to extreme lengths to protect our republic. And second, you will be sick and tired of the inside of a Turkish prison long before we have to release you. Our emergency powers are already set to three months, but we envisage they will last for more than a year as we process the tens of thousands of people being imprisoned in connection with the failed coup.'

The female soldier spoke. 'You have taken enough of our time, Jessica. We want to release and deport you as soon as possible. Please help us to help you.'

Jessica eased-up her thin cotton shirt to reveal the deep blue and purple bruise left by the soldier on her previous visit.

'Absolutely, love. I fully understand that you have my best interests at heart.'

The female soldier continued. 'You know Albay Salepci and Cavus Salepci?'

'Go on.'

The female switched on the tape-recorder, fixed against the wall below a large built-in mirror. After several seconds, the tape-recorder bleeped to notify the two tapes were synchronised. The female soldier introduced herself and the officer introduced himself. Jessica remained silent so that the female introduced her to the tape. Jessica then spoke.

'And an English man is sat in the corner, my guess is Military Intelligence. Let's call him Bond, James Bond.'

The man smiled a silent acknowledgment to Jessica.

'Jessica Khan. Reading your journal, you had relationships with Albay and Cavus Salepci, who are under investigation for treason and other criminal activities. We have been monitoring Albay for some time – and then suddenly Cavus arrived at your door. We believe you aided and abetted these two men and others, in crimes against The Republic Of Turkey. But today we invite you, under caution, to explain why our suspicions may be unfounded. Numerous other offenses, including resisting arrest and assaulting soldiers of the Jandarma, will be considered at a later date. I am, however, authorised to inform you that your cooperation with the more serious acts of terrorism against our country will offset any lesser crimes you committed in the, shall we say, heat of the moment.'

'Terrorism? You are joking! I am saying nothing further, without legal representation.'

The officer spoke in Turkish to the tape-recorder before switching it off. 'Ok Jessica. My colleague will show you to the canteen, you can stay there until your transport arrives. Pleased to have met you.' He stood to leave.

'Transport to where?'

He left the room as the female soldier helped Jessica to her feet and led her down the corridor to a large canteen. Two soldiers sat in one corner. In the centre of the room sat a man, bruised, bloodied and handcuffed.

'*Kizim.*'

'Albay!'

Jessica crossed the room. Albay stood wearily and offered her a weak smile. She smiled back before slapping him with such force that he fell backward onto the floor, knocking away his empty chair. The soldiers did not react.

Rolling onto his cuffed hands, Albay helped himself upright again. Jessica set her jaw and glared at him without moving, as he ran his fingers through her hair and then over her whole body.

'They have not bugged me, Albay. Why are they letting us meet?'

'Mind games, *kizim*. They wind you up and you trip over your own feet. They let you see the enemy and you blurt out information. They are probably eavesdropping now, but more importantly, they want you to change sides.'

'Change fucking sides! How dare you? You ordered Cavus to kill me. You pig!'

'*Kizim*, so far their plan is working, you are already singing. You tell them as much as you like, but don't be cutting your nose to spite your face. I don't really care, I think I am going nowhere, whatever you tell them.'

Jessica turned to leave. Albay took her hand. She stood still to hear what he had to say but did not make eye contact.

'*Disi aslant*. Is he dead?'

Jessica spoke in a low whisper. '*Evet aslanim*. He is dead.'

The soldiers ignored Jessica as she left the canteen. Outside stood the female soldier who followed Jessica back to the interview room.

Jessica stood close to the mirror, inspecting her cuts and bruises. Taking a step forward, she pulled her shirt into a hood and clamped her face to the glass with cupped hands – excluding all light and seeing into the dimly lit room behind the mirror. The Englishman looked back at her.

'If that prick introduces himself and you bring my phone in here, I will tell you everything.'

Jessica sat back into her chair and waited. The female did not answer, but shortly afterward a phone fixed next to the tape-recorder rang. She listened to the voice and left the room. The Englishman entered and handed Jessica her phone. Jessica texted Amara, and the two waited for the return call.

'Jess, what is going on?'

'Am, you are on speakerphone. Are you recording this, please? I am in Koyaka Jandarma, but they are going to move me. I am with some British spook. I am going to tell him everything that just happened to me.' She raised her eyebrows at the man.

'My name is James. I am a security advisor working for the British Consulate in Istanbul.'

Jessica began. 'I met a Turkish guy in Portsmouth; Albay. I believe he slipped me a tracking device. We slept together in Greece. He gave me a box to look after. I met a soldier in Koyaka called Cavus and we had sex, as well. I now believe they were related.'

The Englishman spoke. '*Were* related?'

'Are related. Cavus took something from the box. I did not see what it was. He returned and someone, *this lot*, attacked us. I fought back in self-defence. Your female Jandarma friend threatened to kill me. Cavus returned later and said he would take me to safety. He insisted I go with him; he made me. We kayaked to the end of the peninsula. Two men, presumably Turkish or Greek Special Forces, arrived in a boat from Kos and took him away. I was scared, so I ran away and managed to get back here to seek protection. I know nothing else. He is a soldier, they are all soldiers. I had and have no idea who is a good guy and who is a bad guy. I am a victim.'

'And you killed a serving soldier who you admit to having sex with.'

'No. I did not.'

'They found him dead, in your kayak.'

'News to me. I am not his keeper. Ask the other two guys what happened to him.'

'There was a gunfight. There is blood from two other people and Cavus's discarded firearm.'

'I rest my case. Sounds like Cavus and his mates fell out.'

'Your fingerprints, blood and DNA are on the gun.'

Jessica took an involuntary gulp.

'We played with the gun.' Her face reddened into a deep and embarrassed blush, but she kept her chin up and maintained eye contact.

'Played?'

'We used it as a sex toy. It scratched my leg and maybe inside me. It may also have my saliva on it. I can show you the scratch on my leg. I insist on a civilian medic with warm, small hands to examine elsewhere, if you think that is really necessary.'

'Why did you do that, with the gun?'

'Why not?'

'Your grey dress has gunshot residue on it.'

'My pearly linen dress, if you don't mind. I fired the gun.'

'Why didn't you just say that?'

'I just did say that. We were at the waterfall. He let me shoot a crow.'

'So you can take my friends to the waterfall and show them the remains of a dead crow?'

'No, I missed.'

'Where the empty shell casings fell, then? Where we might find some residue at the firing site.'

Jessica held his gaze.

'Sure, why not? I don't know if that is possible though, I was stood up to my knees in running water at the time, near the waterfall. I guess you might find the bullets away in the hills or the empty casings bobbing around the river or out at sea.'

'That is unfortunate then, Jessica.' She shrugged. 'There is little to corroborate your story.'

'And even less to disprove it then, James.'

James took her phone, swiping it closed. The two looked at each other without expression until the female soldier returned. James left with the phone.

'Jessica!' Netter ran from the camper. 'What is happening?'

Jessica crossed the road carrying an evidence bag containing her house documents and journal.

'I'm not sure, Netter. I am not under arrest, but they will arrest me if I try to leave. Thank you for waiting. I think they have nothing on me for anything, other than some serious assaults against the soldiers. Slightly exaggerated if you ask me – they accuse me of assault, attempting to steal a firearm, assisting a fugitive to escape and believe it or not, keeping a dangerous dog.

'The way I see it, they trapped me in a brawl between various soldiers, I tried to defend myself from injury, I accidentally kicked a soldier's hand away from his pistol and the fucking dog isn't even mine; it belongs to their Village Headman.

'You want to hear something really funny? It seems I actually bought the shack – I own a house on the sunny Aegean.' Jessica raised the evidence bag containing the house documents. 'Every cloud, eh? My biggest concern is why they want me out of custody. What do they want to happen to me, away from their *protection*, or at least away from their complicity?'

They drove the short distance to the shack. Parked across the road from the bed-and-breakfast sat two soldiers in a Jandarma van, the lights flashing. Elvis slowly wagged his thick, heavy tail against the veranda as Jessica and her friends stepped over him. Jessica returned to the Jandarma van with two mugs of coffee and a plate of sweet, sticky baklava.

'Hey guys. For you. And turn the flashing lights off, there's a sweetie.'

The driver obliged and Jessica returned to the picnic table where Belgi and Netter sat with beers. As soon as Elvis heard her voice, he made his way over to lie on her feet.

'Ok. So here is the plan. You leave me a phone, they still have mine. I start making calls in the morning, you two head away from here and if I was you, out of Turkey.'

Belgi replied. 'We go nowhere, kid. Our plan is – you stop fighting the Turkish Army at every opportunity, we stay here until you get your passport and then we all leave together.'

'Look…'

'No Jessica, you look.' Netter spoke over Jessica. 'Belgi told you what we are doing. It is not up to you. *Compris*?'

Jessica nodded. 'Ok. Thank you. I need a couple of beers. Then let's go to bed.'

'See! You are right, Netter. She changed her mind.'

Both women grinned at the reference, but Netter slapped his arm, anyway.

CHAPTER 14 – FRIENDS ARMS

Heat from the noon sun woke Jessica; her friends had slept in the camper. She felt hungry and thirsty from the long sleep. Taking a glass of water, she headed out of the shack towards voices and the group stood and sat around the picnic table. As her eyes adjusted to the bright sun, she froze mid-stride. Elvis walked blindly into the back of her legs and sat.

Amara was showing her passport to the Jandarma. Stacy sat at the table with Belgi and Netter. Stacy wore a slinky satin trouser suit in maroon and an emerald green hijab.

At first, nobody moved except for the Jandarma looking between Jessica and the group.

'Amara. Fancy. On holiday?'

Amara let her passport fall to the ground for the Jandarma to retrieve. The closer she came to Jessica, the more her face contorted into an expression of concern and horror. Amara's eyes welled as she ran a finger over Jessica's dry and split lips, the cuts and bruises across her face and the grazes down the side of her temples and chin. Jessica wore a short T-shirt and briefs for bed, Amara saw the bruising where the soldier had kicked her. She wore thin white sports socks and fluffy slippers over her swollen feet.

'Jess. My God, you look…'

'Yeah, I know socks and slippers are not my best look. But Stacy looks dafter.'

Amara glanced over her shoulder at Stacy, waving from the picnic table. She managed a thin smile.

'Don't ask. She thinks she is a bloody Sultana. She chose to ignore my dress advice. She's as kinky as you are.'

Amara led Jessica away from the others and with Elvis, the three sat on the veranda.

'Jessica, I am really worried…'

'Am, they are going to kill me.'

'Who?'

'Them.' Jessica made an expansive gesture with her right arm. 'The Turks. The army, the rebels, the British, the Greeks. They are queuing up like that scene from the Airplane film. Quite funny, really. I think I may have overstepped the mark this time. I tried to kill the president, I killed a Turkish soldier and shot a couple of Greek Special Forces. There is a British spy following me around the country. I can seriously embarrass NATO, let alone grass-up the rebels. I am struggling to think who doesn't want me dead, to be honest. The Embassy has stopped taking my calls – they say they are transferring me, but the line goes dead.' She watched Elvis panting in the sun. 'Even the dog's owner has gone off me. Whoever gets the opportunity first will do the others a favour. Nobody is on my side. Nobody wants me in court. You always said I was reckless.'

Amara whispered her reply, barely able to form the words.

'My love. I am hearing the same from my security people at work. Not the assassination bit obviously, but it is difficult to find anyone to speak positively about your situation.'

'Amara. I don't want to die.'

'I know, sweetheart. I know.'

The two embraced.

Stacy slinked over, acting the Queen Of Sheba.

'Hey, babes. Been in the wars?' She pulled the hijab across her face and batted her eyes at the

Jandarma, who both smiled. 'So, are you under arrest? House arrest? I assume you do not have your passport.' Stacy annoyingly preened and flirted with the Jandarma as Jessica spoke.

'No, not really. I suppose I can walk to the cafes or the beach looking like a punch bag, but I can't travel anywhere without ID. And as you can see, I have a couple of guys looking after me.'

Stacy covered her mouth and nose with her hijab, lowering her eyes coyly at the soldiers – morphing from Queen Of Sheba into Helen Of Troy.

'So babe. Let's see inside your villa, I just love what I've seen on Facebook.' Amara and Jessica made eye contact. Amara managed a weak smile, and Jessica shook her head.

'Whatever Stace.'

As the three women entered the shack, Stacy took a long glance at the soldiers from over her shoulder – now playing the Harlot from Arabian Nights. One Jandarma nudged the other and they returned to sit on the road curb, in the shade of their van and the bougainvillea growing from the hotel garden.

An hour passed with Belgi and Netter relaxing in the shade at the picnic table. The two Jandarma played backgammon and Elvis sat facing the shack door. All faces turned as it opened and the visitors stepped onto the veranda. They spoke for a few moments before both hugging their friend, now wearing her white fluffy onesie and towel drying her hair with an oversized beach-sheet.

The visitors linked arms and walked to the hire car, speaking briefly to Netter and Belgi on the way. Elvis followed the two women, his nose only inches from their legs. Amara then strode to the Jandarma.

'Passports, please. We are going to Bodrum to collect our bags from the hotel and then we are booking-in here.' Amara pointed to the Bed-and-Breakfast. 'Anything happens to her while we are away and I will hold you responsible, understood?'

The Jandarma respectfully stood and saluted as Amara approached, but neither were impressed by her hollow threats. Amara continued.

'Leave her to sleep, understood? And if you need anything from her, I want a female officer to go in, understood? And not that nasty, violent bitch that kicked her! She is feeling unwell and needs to sleep.'

'Unwell Miss? What is the problem?' The Jandarma made to walk to the shack.

'She has her period.' Both men stopped. 'And it is very heavy.'

'Oh. Ok, Miss.'

'She is tired but when she lies down the blood is so thick and sticky…'

The younger of the Jandarma held a hand to silence Amara.

'It is ok, Miss. We will leave her to rest. No problem. See you later perhaps.'

Amara returned to the hire car, gave a last wave to the shack, Netter and Belgi before pulling onto the road. The Jandarma saw the Queen Of Sheba already sleeping in the reclined passenger seat.

The female officer arrived with two other soldiers at shift change. The sun had dipped and only the fairy lights Jessica hung around her bed provided illumination from the shack. The female soldier ticked a document attached to a clipboard and made a few notes.

'*No other visitors? She hasn't spoken to you? What has she been doing all afternoon?*' She sounded bored and irritated by her own questions.

'*We have been keeping a close eye on her through the screen door.*' The younger soldier held-up binoculars and smirked at his older colleague. The female bristled.

The older colleague spoke, clearing his throat.

'*She has changed into her sleeping hoodie suit. She has been moving around a little, but mostly she lies down, reading. I think she is very tired and maybe it is not a good time of the month for her.*'

The female nodded, looking towards the campervan. Netter sat on the step of the open camper reading Belgi's Lads Reunited book, whilst Belgi sat at the table with a beer, scratching Elvis's ears.

The female soldier spoke. '*How long has the dog been with them?*'

'*All afternoon. It is too hot for him...*'

'*Why isn't he on the veranda or facing the door?*'

The two soldiers shrugged.

The four shift soldiers followed the female's stride to the shack. She pushed open the screen door and barged in without knocking. Startled, Stacy sprung to her feet, facing the soldier.

'Where is she?' the soldier shouted.

'Jessica? With Amara. Bodrum I guess, I don't know. They should be back soon. She isn't under arrest or anything.'

The soldier took a step forward, pushing Stacy against the wall.

'What have you done?'

'Nothing. I wanted to chill here. I've done nothing wrong. Your guys saw her leave.'

The older of the soldiers spoke in Turkish. *'She had this woman's hijab on. We didn't see her face.'*

'In your clothes, bitch?'

'She is self-conscious of her injuries, so she borrowed my hijab. She is awfully vain. I mean, I know she is pretty and everything…'

The female soldier grabbed Stacy's throat and lifted her from the floor, against the wall. Stacy tried to throw a punch, but barely impacted the soldier's shoulder. She felt her eyes bulging with pressure, she could not breathe, agonising pain shot through her larynx and sinuses. Her sight faded as the ringing in her ears intensified. The soldier's nose pushed against her own.

'You bitch. What have you done?'

Stacy felt her bladder empty down her leg. Her flaying hands made contact with the chest of the older soldier. He had one hand against the female soldier and the other firmly pulled at the hand around Stacy's throat.

'Let her go. That is enough now, you are going to kill her. Let her go.'

Stacy felt the grip loosen enough for her to take a rasping breath and then her released body slipped down the wall, as she struggled not to blackout. She saw Netter pushing past the soldiers.

Amara and Jessica queued in the packed ferry departure hall. Passport control pulled Turkish passport holders from the line – they needed written authority to leave the country and their documents were being scrutinised by border guards, passport control and the police. Tempers frayed and passport controllers processing the tourists and ex-pats, also watched the Turkish section closely, in case the situation flared out of control.

The border guard told Jessica to pull back her hijab and then to pull it from her hair.

'Hair colour?'

'Yes, this is natural. Photo is from years ago.'

'What happened to your face?'

'Road accident. Knocked off a scooter in Bodrum. You all drive like maniacs.'

The border guard moved from behind his desk and held the passport open against Jessica's face for comparison. There was a scream from the Turkish section and all heads turned. The guard held the passport to Jessica's face for several more seconds, but his attention was across the room. He returned to his desk, scanned the biometrics and stamped the visa; waving them through to board the ferry.

'We need to check on Stacy. I can't believe you guys have done all this for me.'

'This is where it gets complicated, Vanilla. Our Company insurance, including legal, covers Stacy and me for private travel, but not you obviously. So I have arranged for the Company's nominated insurance lawyer and a guy from the consulate to meet me in Kos and of course, you will happen to be with me. I have explained that our friend is in trouble, and I felt the need to flee the Jandarma for my own safety. The Greeks, Brits, EU, NATO and the yanks are all a bit twitchy about the Turkey situation – especially as they would have welcomed a successful coup. The US is already reluctantly involved by harbouring Gulen, who may have helped organise the coup. Turkey is hugely important to the west in Syria and everyone wants Turkey to be a strong and stable partner in the region. The last thing they want is Brits running around on false passports, avoiding the legitimate Turkish authorities. Or worse – Brits being involved in the coup and assassinations – young lady.

'We will be whisked away to Blighty on an emergency passport for you, as you *lost* yours. The consulate in Izmir is driving down with a replacement passport for Stacy, who will report hers missing as soon as I text to say we are in Greek waters. Our legal-rep in Turkey is also going to meet her, in case her passport *may* have been used to commit some crime, or other.

'And to answer your question, sweetheart, Stacy will be fine. She is as cool as a cucumber; most of this is her idea.'

Jessica nodded. She made to speak, but Amara spoke over her.

'Jess, you are in serious danger and getting you home and away from the region is just the start of keeping you safe. But start we must.'

Jessica nodded again, watching her own hands wring themselves on autopilot.

The late afternoon sun sat low in the sky and illuminated the waves into a million diamonds. The ferry manoeuvred close to the jut of rock where Jessica had fought three Special Forces soldiers, probably from two different armies, and won. She remembered the accepting expression on Cavus's face as he fell to his death from the cliff. Amara hugged her close as Jessica shivered.

'Poor fool. He thought I loved him.'

'Who?'

'Just some guy in a uniform. Did I tell you Am, I met a real hunk when I was hiking the Cinque Terre? Pass me my journal, please. I will call him, his number is on a post-it.'

'Nice guy, no complications?'

'He might be queer and married to a man called Kris, I'm not sure. But other than that...'

The two women sat in silence as the boat passed the crime scene to their left. Amara watched Jessica tense.

'I got you this.' Amara reached into her bag and offered Jessica a paperback, along with the journal, trying to distract her.

'Salep and Ginger by Jane Gundogan. Thanks.' A note in Amara's handwriting read:

To my love, Jessica,
Fall back into your friend's arms
Love,
Amara

'That is the characters' names, Salep and Ginger; I have had a quick flick through. It is so funny, exactly your humour. It is about a girl with a broken heart that tries to fix it in Turkey. I don't know why I thought of you.'

The women smiled.

'Salep and ginger is also a drink. For the winter mostly, but good following a shock. Albay...'

The ferry slowed to ease past a Turkish Coastguard cutter. A Navy gunner manned the Bren-gun fixed to the roof of the bridge. Five-hundred meters away sat a Greek frigate – engines exhausting smoke, static in the swell. The gunner laid an oily cloth over the machinegun firing mechanism and had stretched a condom over the muzzle to protect the barrel from salt spray. Cavus and Jessica had not used condoms during their lovemaking, but seeing the gun *sexualised* made her catch her breath.

Amara realised the paperback was not enough to distract Jessica – she could not allow a meltdown, especially while still in Turkish waters.

'You've lots of calls to make Jess. Chris is worried sick and he says your neighbour is talking to your old landlord about getting back the flat. Jess?' In a last-ditch attempt to distract Jessica, Amara added, 'Stacy said Chris's new girlfriend is really gorgeous.'

It did not work.

'Am, he's going to shoot me.'

Jessica watched the cutter lurch in the swell. The ferry lost manoeuvrability as it slowed to pass the cutter and the two vessels now bobbed dangerously close, the cutter rising high in the water above the side of the ferry. The gunner steadied the Bren as coastguard sailors moved to the bow to fend off contact with the ferry. The commotion unfolded immediately outside Jessica's window.

'Jess, look at me. Nobody is shooting anybody. Look at me and breathe. You need to stay calm, people are looking.'

The cutter crashed down onto the side of the ferry. Several people shouted from around the ferry saloon. One young man screamed and the ferry captain sounded a long blast on the ship's horn. Jessica looked into the eyes of the gunner before noticing Greek Navy ribs full of marines heading towards the stricken ferry. Jessica screamed and tried to clamber past Amara and away from the gunner. Amara grabbed at Jessica, pulling her close. Jessica screamed again.

'Amara move, he is going to shoot me!'

Amara restrained Jessica against the row of seats in front. Feeling her seat being kicked and punched by a screaming Jessica, a teenage girl turned around and grasped her flaying hands, reassuring Jessica in soothing tones. A middle-aged couple from the row behind leaned forward, the man massaged the nape of Jessica's neck as his wife smoothed her hair.

Amara spoke to the audience. 'She has a phobia of drowning.'

The teenager translated and several people sighed and murmured reassuring words. Jessica forced herself to relax, making a low nasal groan through gritted teeth in an effort to control her breathing. She felt the soothing hands from behind and squeezed hard on the girl's hands from in front. She imagined Albay reassuring her - *you are never alone in Turkey.*

The damaged ferry limped into port at half speed. Amara helped Jessica ashore, holding her close. Border Control waved them through, stopping only Turks to check passports. Amara read a text message, which had bleeped on to her phone, and replied as she spoke.

'Your Jandarma friend gave Stacy a bit of a slap, but no damage done. The lawyer has called to say he will be with her shortly. I expect she will be home in England before us.'

Jessica nodded. Amara pointed to a black people carrier. Two suits stood at the open backdoors and two others in jeans scanned the area around the dock.

'What do you think Jessica, our taxi?' Jessica nodded again. 'Come on Vanilla, penny for your thoughts.'

'Nothing much, Am. I was just wondering if I could sneak back into Turkey on Stacy's old passport and collect my car. It would be quite an adventure; fancy tagging along?

'Why is that so funny, Amara? I was going to leave it a few weeks, obviously!'

2016 - The Start Of My New Life

1. Work ✓ - Finished at the Company. Take a long break and then find something I love to do; helping people or looking after animals. Rabbits or Blind Dogs.

2. Chris ✓ - Moved on from Chris. Take back control of my life. Make my own decisions. Don't lean on Amara, now that Chris has gone.
Lean on me as much as you want, my love!

3. Flat ✓ - Moved on. Buy or rent bigger, or maybe ask Landlord for my tiny flat back if new tenants cannot squeeze in.

4. *Travel Europe* ✓ *A Road Trip. Thelma And Louise. (Or just Thelma). And beyond Europe.*

5. *Make awesome new friends* ✓ *for life*

6. *Wild Camp* ✓ *And go wild*

7. *Meet a rich, handsome, guy* ✓ *your own age! Maybe more mature Fall in love Or lust!*

8. *Stay in the poshest ever boutique hotel and pamper myself* ✓ *and buy a holiday home – aim for the stars*

9. *Swim in a waterfall* ✓ *and be dried by the sun or a hunk*

10. *Just Live A Little* ✓ *and stay safe Or at least stay alive*

11. *Prioritise myself* ✓ *over and above anyone else – you are the most important*

12. *Wear a soldier's uniform and fire his gun* ✓ *kinky! fight him for it first* ✓

13. Fall back into your friend's arms – I will always be ready to catch you ✓

Be careful what you wish for

Acknowledgements:

Jane Gundogan
Max Speed
Pamdiana Jones

for literary inspiration

Amanda Sherridan

for inspiration, mentoring (and the cover design
for Covid Blues And Twos)

Paul McMurrough

for all of the above and the cover design for
Listless In Turkey

Printed in Great Britain
by Amazon